# Jonathan Park
### & the
# Secret of the Hidden Cave

Lloyd R. Hight

# Jonathan Park

## & the Secret of the Hidden Cave

written by
**Sandy & Pat Roy**

illustrated by Lloyd R. Hight

Master
Books

First printing: June 1999

ISBN: 0-89051-263-9
Library of Congress Number: 99-64019

Cover design by Janell Robertson
Illustrations by Ron L. Hight

**Printed in the United States of America.**

To our ten-year-old *Jonathan* Roy. . . .

Because of your love for dinosaurs, we
wanted to write this adventure for children
everywhere. We look forward to the adventures
*we'll* share in the future. And because of our love,
we dedicate this book to you.

# Contents

# 1

# Journey into the Storm

T he red 4x4 sped down the muddy road, spraying water from newly formed streams. While his father, Kendall, navigated the unpaved road, ten-year-old Jonathan Park held tightly to the dashboard as the truck dipped and pitched . The windshield wipers flopped helplessly back and forth, unable to keep up with the driving rain. It was a race against time.

"The clouds are getting darker!" Jonathan yelled above the noise.

The sky flashed, temporarily blinding the two as they strained to see through the windshield. A clap of thunder boomed through the noise of the storm. "If we could just make it to Ghost Ranch before dark. It was a mistake to wait for a break in the storm," said Kendall. "I'm sorry, Jonathan, I shouldn't have dragged you out in this!" Hail began pelting the car as if to emphasize his point.

"Dad, it's okay," Jonathan said, thinking more about their present situation than what his dad was saying.

"It never rains like this! But this week, when I finally get the okay to investigate Ghost Ranch, it pours," Kendall fumed, "and now we've wasted time on this dead-end road. It looked like a short cut on the map." Looking through the windshield, he could barely make out the towering layered cliffs in the distance — their earth-colored hues blurred by the storm. Then a more serious thought occurred to him. *With this much rain, they must be letting millions of gallons of water over Abiquiu Dam!*

They looked down to the left at the small river they had recently crossed. The tiny stream at the bottom of the hill had become a swirling mass of red mud carrying anything in its path as it crept up the steep banks.

Suddenly, a large bolt of lightning flashed across the road, igniting a tree just a few hundred feet ahead of the truck. The blast of power tossed the smoldering tree on to the road in front of them, blocking their path. "Dad!" yelled Jonathan. "Watch out!"

"Hold on, Jonathan!" Kendall Park had a split second to determine which path to take. To the right a high bank rose beside them, to the left was a steep ravine, but the 4x4 might be able to make it. He pulled the wheel severely to the left. At first the truck didn't respond. The front wheels spun, throwing mud onto the windshield and blurring their vision as the truck slid toward the tree. Then the front tires dug in, spinning the truck around. The back end caught a fallen log, sending the truck over the edge toward the rising river.

They both screamed as the 4x4 slid, head first, down the muddy embankment! The truck came to a quick stop when the front right bumper thumped against a tree, spinning them 180 degrees. It was quiet for a moment except for the sound of the windshield wipers, the rain, and the two of them breathing heavily.

"Son, are you okay?"

"Yeah, I'm okay, Dad."

They looked at each other and smiled nervously, a little shaken from their ride.

"So much for Ghost Ranch," Jonathan's dad sighed in defeat. "Let's just see if we can get out of here. I hope the engine starts again." He turned the key. The starter clicked several times and then was silent. "Just great!" he said, hitting the wheel. Then calming himself he added, "I'm getting out to check the damage."

"Okay." Jonathan watched as his dad took his felt-brimmed hat from the seat. In the midst of danger, Jonathan looked at his father's face. His dad's sky-blue eyes and determined jaw reflected

a quiet confidence that calmed his fears.

Kendall placed his hat on his short, strawberry blond hair, and then, as always, adjusted it so it hung just above his eyes. "That's a steep embankment we came down, but the 4x4 should be able to make it," he said. Rain poured in as he opened the door. "I'll see if I can get it to work. Hop into the driver's side and turn the key when I say to, okay, Jonathan?"

"Okay, Dad," Jonathan said as he slid behind the wheel. He turned his baseball cap to the back, pushed up the sleeves on his denim jacket, and then sat with his hand on the key, poised for action. Except for the light blond hair poking out of his cap, he was the image of his father.

Jonathan watched intently as his dad opened the hood and tugged on the battery cables.

"Okay, give it a try."

Jonathan turned the key. The starter clicked and then stopped.

"How about now?" Kendall shouted above the storm. The starter clicked one more time, and then went silent. Kendall took a deep breath, then exhaled. As the water rolled from his hat to his face, he felt older than his 38 years. "Okay, I'm gonna try to find a way up that hill to see if I can see any nearby ranches," Kendall said pointing to the steep bank above the road. "Stay here for a minute."

"But, Dad. . . ."

"No buts. I may need you to call for help, so just stay put!" Jonathan's dad turned to look at the task ahead of him and took deep a breath.

The air was filled with the damp smell of rain. Kendall was at the bottom of the ravine staring up at tall, slender aspen trees. Their ghostly, white trunks held up golden crowns of fall leaves fluttering in the wind. Raindrops beat against them on their way to the ground. The sound of the rain and the howling wind played a haunting melody, causing Kendall to feel small and alone. He shivered, his body betraying his resolve to remain strong.

Kendall grabbed at bushes as he made his way up the steep embankment. Little streams of water flowed over the hill, washing mud over his boots and going up his coat sleeves. He made it to the road where the truck had slid off. He stood for a moment, looking at the tire tracks in the mud, then continued to climb. "Just a few more feet and I'll be up to that rock," he coached himself, continuing up the hillside. He reached a ledge ten feet across and four feet wide. "Or this will do," he breathed. He sat down and leaned back against the hillside to rest. Suddenly, the hillside gave way, and he found himself tumbling downward into darkness.

"Wh . . . whoa . . . Jonathan!" Kendall's voice echoed as he slid down a chute through a giant opening in the ground!

From inside the truck, Jonathan saw his dad disappear from sight. "Dad!" Jonathan yelled. He flung the door open and jumped out into the rain, his boots splashing mud on his faded jeans. "Daadddd!" His voice echoed into the canyon, and then all was quiet. "Dad, where are you?"

Meanwhile, just a few miles away, the Brenan family was fighting their own battle in the storm.

Jim Brenan threw on his boots and rain poncho. "I'm gonna check on the river, Martha," he said to his wife on his way out the door.

"Call me on the CB," Martha cried out.

"Right," Jim said over his shoulder. Then, pausing for a moment, he turned in the doorway and said, "I love you."

"I love you, too!" Martha said with a catch in her throat. He didn't say those words often, so she knew the situation was serious. Martha looked around, wondering for a moment where to begin. From the mischievous dark-haired beauty that married Jim, to the more round, down-to-earth woman she was now, she'd always been confident in her role as a farmer's wife. And now there was a possibility of losing it all. She paused for a minute, standing there in her elastic waist jeans and oversized sweatshirt. For the first time she could remember in her 33 years, Martha felt lost.

The dog barked behind Jim as he stepped from the porch into the storm.

"Okay, c'mon, Shadow," Jim said, opening the door of the battered, blue Chevy pickup.

The dog wagged his tail and jumped into the passenger side as the engine roared to life.

Jim skirted the swollen river at the north end of his property, gunning the engine. He stopped and got out to survey the area with Shadow right behind him. The water was about to overflow the banks of the river.

"We gotta go boy, c'mon!" said Jim turning to get back into the pick-up. Shadow had crept out on a log that hung over the river. "Hey, Shadow, watch out!" Jim heard a loud crack as the log broke under Shadow's weight. Shadow tried to back up, but the branch was swept down the river, taking the dog with it.

"Shadow!" Jim shouted rushing to the river's edge. Shadow barked and paddled wildly trying to get back to the side. Jim ran beside him along the riverbank, trying to keep up, but the water was carrying the dog so fast Jim soon fell behind. He knew saving Shadow would cost him valuable time he didn't have. With tears in his eyes, Jim ran back to the pickup and started the engine. He grabbed the microphone on his CB. "Martha?"

"I hear you. How does it look?"

"Shadow is lost in the river!" Jim exclaimed into the mike.

"Lost?" Martha repeated in disbelief. "Can't you go after him?" She knew how much Jim loved that dog. She loved him herself.

"There just isn't time!" Jim cried. "The river is rising too fast. Its over the banks. At this rate our crops will be flooded sooner than I thought. Keep the radio on to see what roads are still open. Be ready. I think we'll have to evacuate. I'm on my way back."

In the barn, ten-year-old Jessica Brenan was feeding the last bits of hay to a three month old, light brown Guernsey calf. "Here you go, Molly B."

"Moo!" said the calf, licking her appreciatively.

"Hey, a cow lick! That tickles," Jessie giggled.

A thunderclap broke, echoing throughout the barn. Molly gave a scared "moo" and nuzzled Jessie with her velvety-soft nose. Jessie saw fear in the big brown eyes looking back at her.

"Oh, Molly," Jessie said, kissing the calf and rubbing her neck. "I know it's a scary storm, but you're gonna be all right. You just stay here in the barn until we can take you up to higher ground," she said, turning to leave. Jessie was just latching the barn when she heard her mom's voice in the distance.

"Jessie? Jessie!" Martha yelled above the storm.

"Yeah, Mom?" she yelled back, running up the hill toward the house.

"Are you ready to go?"

"What?" Jessie asked, pulling her coat tight to her neck as she ran against the wind.

"Look at you! You're drenched!" Martha scolded as Jessie

made her way up to the porch. "You need to pack some clothes. Your dad says we may have to evacuate!"

"Evacuate?" Jessie was breathing hard as she entered the house. "But Mom, Dad said I could help him take the new calf to higher ground."

"There's no time for that now, Jessie. The river's rising too fast. We have to be ready to go when your father gets here. Now, get moving!" Martha stood with her hands on her hips, signaling that she meant business.

Jessie could hear the tension in her mother's voice.

— —

Jonathan stood straining to see where his dad had gone. Night was coming quickly, and the sky was made even darker by the storm. He heard a rustle in the bushes and felt as if someone or something was staring at him. Jonathan strained to see the hidden creature. He could only see a black silhouette of the animal that emerged from the bushes. Jonathan heard a low growl. A flash of lightening revealed bared white teeth and yellow eyes creeping toward him. In the next moment, the sky went dark, leaving him alone with the black animal.

— —

At the Brenans', thunder rumbled across the sky. Martha and Jessie heard rain pounding on the roof above. "Oh, I promised your dad I'd listen to the radio. He'll be back soon. . . ." Martha finished the rest of her sentence quietly to herself, "I hope."

Martha turned on the radio, tuning in a station from Santa Fe. She noticed that Jessie hadn't moved. "Jessica Brenan. Don't just stand there!"

"But what about Molly?" said Jessie, her eyes watering.

"I don't know, Jessie," Martha said, softening and giving her a hug.

Loud beeps coming over the radio commanded their attention. Both of them listened to the radio as the tones ended. "The following is an emergency broadcast. Due to the last weeks of severe rain, the U.S. Corps of Engineers has been releasing large amounts of water over Abiquiu Dam. Combined with today's downpour, flash floods are currently overtaking some areas of the county. The following communities are advised to evacuate immediately. If you live in the vicinity of Canones, Barranca, or Abiquiu, you need to leave immediately. Highways 89, 96, and 550 are still open." The radio continued in the background.

"Mom!" Jessie exclaimed, "That's us!"

"Jessie, can you watch for your father from the window?" Martha picked up the phone and dialed. "Mother?" Jessie could hear her grandma's alarmed voice over the phone from where she was standing.

Martha continued, "We're okay, but we have to evacuate. It sounds like the water is coming right through our property!"

"He's coming up onto the front porch!" Jessie announced.

Martha acknowledged Jessie as she continued to talk to her mother on the phone. "Can Ryan stay with you another night? All right. Tell him we'll be there tomorrow afternoon. We'll just stay somewhere safe tonight. Pray for us." Martha paused to hear her mom's answer. "We'll be careful. I'm sure we'll be fine. We love you, too. Bye."

The front door flew open as Jim Brenan stood in the doorway. Rain dripped from his poncho, and he was soaked to the bone. His dark, curly hair was drenched and water trickled from his head onto his broad shoulders. The sound of the storm filled the living room.

"Martha, Martha!" Jim puffed, as he slammed the door. "The creek is rising faster than I've ever seen it!"

"The radio, Dad. . . ."

Martha cut her off. "The radio said we need to evacuate!"

"I know, I heard!" Jim exclaimed. "You ready?"

"What about the animals? I thought we were going to take them to higher ground," said Jessie.

"There just isn't time. We've got to go now!"

"We're ready, I think," said Martha pulling on her yellow rain poncho and picking up their suitcase. "Jessie?"

"I'm ready, Mom. But Molly. . . ."

"Let's go!" Jim said, taking a final look around their home, and grabbing the rest of their things.

Jonathan stood in the rain, shrinking away from the creature growling at him. It was a large, angry black dog. It stood slightly above Jonathan on the hill. Jonathan had to either get past it to get to his dad or retreat to the car. "Whoah! Nice doggie," Jonathan said, backing up as the dog inched forward. "Big doggie." The dog bared its teeth. "Really scary-looking doggie," Jonathan said, as he tried to inch past it. The dog crept closer, gaining its advantage while Jonathan fought back the fear.

Suddenly, Jonathan remembered what his grandpa did when a dog had once cornered him. Grandpa had given the dog his fiercest look, growled back at the dog, and lunged. Jonathan leaned forward and began to growl and bare his teeth. The dog's ears went back and his eyes widened, sizing up the boy. Jonathan lunged and barked. Startled, the dog backed up just enough for Jonathan to get by. Jonathan shot past the dog and pulled his way up the grass toward the hole. He could feel the dog's hot breath on his back and turned around to bark again as fiercely as he could. This time the dog turned and disappeared into the night.

Through the dim light, Jonathan could only see the mouth of the dark hole. Though overgrown with brush, it was about four feet across. "Dad, are you okay?" he yelled into the darkness. He hoped his dad was able to hear him.

"Yes, Jonathan, I'm okay. In fact, it may be better in here than it is out there," Kendall's voice echoed. Jonathan sighed with relief.

"Jonathan, can you go back down to the truck and get a rope and flashlight? I think we should spend the night in here."

"You want me to go back to the truck?" Jonathan asked, thinking of the dog.

"Yes, I know it's a long way, but we'll need those things."

"You don't know the half of it," Jonathan muttered under his breath.

"What?"

"Okay, Dad."

"And, uh, Jonathan?"

"Yes, Dad?" Jonathan yelled back down the hole.

"Call your mom on the cell phone and let her know we're all right."

"Okay." Jonathan ran and slid down the hill to the truck. He looked around, but the dog had disappeared for the moment.

"Look how high the water's getting!" Jim yelled over the storm. He, Martha, and Jessie ran down the steps of the porch and across the lawn to the muddy driveway. A small group of ducks scattered as the Brenan family splashed through the deep puddles.

As they reached the car, Martha looked back beyond the barn. "Jim, look!" She yelled, "It's already to our crops!"

"Everyone in the car, right now!" Jim ordered.

The wind blew violently against Jessie, making it hard to open the door. It shut behind her with a slam, muffling the sounds of the storm.

"If we don't get out of here right now, the water is going to catch us! Where are the keys?" Jim said, settling into the seat.

"Jim, don't you have them?" Martha asked, panicked, as she rustled through her purse.

Behind them, the electrical box on the side of the barn burst into a ball of sparks and electrical arcs. "What was that!" yelled Jessie.

The lights of the barn flashed, then went out. In his rearview mirror, Jim saw the flash and then darkness filled the night. "For Pete's sake, the water's already reached the barn! Where's the keys?"

"Molly!" said Jessie in distress. "She's in there, Dad! We've got to get her out!"

"It's too late, Jessie. I'm sorry, but we've got to save ourselves. She and all the animals are in God's hands now."

Jessie strained to see out the back window into the darkening scene. "Dad, I see the water coming toward us!" she screamed.

Jim turned on the car's inside light and frantically searched for the keys.

"The keys aren't in my purse!" cried Martha. "You just had them!"

"We're doomed!" Jim exclaimed, "There's no way to outrun the water without the car!"

Suddenly Jessie spotted something shiny. "Dad, the keys are in the ignition."

"Praise God!" Jim said with sincerity.

"Oh, for cryin' out loud," said Martha.

Jim turned the key. The engine cranked over, sputtered, and then died. "Not now!"

"Dad! There's water coming through the door!" Jessie shrieked. She looked out to see water all around the car.

"Dear Lord, please help us!" Jim prayed as he turned the key again. The engine roared to life. He said a quick prayer of thanks.

———✦———

In the darkening skies, it was getting harder for Jonathan to see. As rain continued to pour, little streams rushed down the hill past the red 4x4. Just then the entire sky lit up with a brilliant flash followed by a crack of thunder. Inside the truck, Jonathan found the cell phone and called Angela Park. "Mom? Mom!"

"Jonathan, thank the Lord you're okay! Is your dad okay? Where are you?"

"We're on, actually just off of, highway 89, 50 miles north of Santa Fe."

"Are you by Abiquiu reservoir?" she asked.

"Yeah, kinda. Just below it."

"I knew it! You've got to get out of that area. They're having everyone evacuate! The dam's overflowing." The cell phone began to break up.

"We're kind of stuck, Mom."

"Stuck? Jonathan what happened? Where's your father?"

"The truck went down an embankment. And then Dad slid down a hole."

"A hole!" Angela cried out in horror. "Jonathan, is your dad all right?"

"Yeah, Mom, Dad's all right. The hole is a cave, and it's right in the hills above route 162. Dad thinks it's a good place to sit out the storm," Jonathan explained.

"Are you going to be. . . ." the voice on the phone broke up.

"Mom, send someone to get us!" Jonathan pleaded.

"Jonathan, where are. . . ." The voice never finished.

"Mom! Mom! Can you hear me?" Jonathan yelled in desperation. "Mom?" There was no answer.

———✦———

The Brenans' car sped along a muddy road, up the hill, the headlights cutting through the darkness of the stormy night.

"Poor Molly," said Jessie quietly, as if in shock. She thought of the helpless calf that had trusted her so fearlessly. Jessie herself had sealed Molly's doom by latching the door of the barn. She tried to push the thought out of her mind before guilt set in.

Martha was looking into the side mirror. "Jim, the water's still behind us! Are we going to get up high enough?"

"If we can just make it up a little higher, the water will spill down into the ravine. Then we'll skirt along our property until we make it to safety," Jim explained.

"Our farm!" exclaimed Martha, the weight of how much could be lost hitting her. She knew that their home, their livelihood, their simple, good way of living could be gone even now.

"Honey, I think we have to trust the Lord. Let's not think about it now," consoled Jim.

"How are we going to make it without our grape crops?" Martha worried.

"Mom," said Jessie weakly, "God will take care of us, won't He?" Jessie's mom was usually so full of confidence. It made Jessie nervous to see her so upset.

Martha looked back to see a younger version of herself reflected in Jessie's earnest gaze. Jessie's big, hazel eyes were different from Martha's deep-set, dark blue beauties, but they normally carried the same confident twinkle that Martha understood. Now Martha saw her own fears mirrored in Jessie's stare. At once she pushed those anxious thoughts out of her head and looked at Jessie. "He always has, hasn't He?" she said, playfully tugging on Jessie's braid. "I just. . . ."

Jim cut her off. "Hold on!" Through the rain-drenched windshield, Jim saw a huge tree in the path of the headlights.

"Watch out!" shouted Jessie.

"Oh dear Lord, please help us!" prayed Martha.

Jim instantly hit the brakes, and the Brenan car slid to a stop, inches from the fallen tree. "I can't believe this! Now what are we supposed to do?" As he looked out his window, dim flashing yellow lights caught his attention. The tone of his voice changed. "Hey. . . there's a truck down there in the ravine."

—◆—

"Now that's what I call a warm fire, right, Jonathan?" Kendall's voice echoed in the hollowness of the cave.

"Yeah," agreed Jonathan.

In the flickering light of the fire, Jonathan looked at the cave around him. From where he was sitting he could barely see the mouth of the cave. The opening was a narrow slippery chute that cut diagonally through the mountain. The chute went for about ten feet, getting steeper as as it neared the floor of the cave. Once inside, the cave opened up to a large circular room about 20 feet across and 10 feet high. A dark opening signaled that the cave continued past the room. Jonathan's observations were interrupted by his dad.

"So, your mom said they're evacuating this area. I was afraid of that. They're letting too much water out of Abiquiu Dam. Well, son, we have two options: We could brave the storm outside or stay here for the time being. And this looks like the better choice."

"I put the hazard lights on the truck, but I'm not sure anyone will see 'em," said Jonathan.

"Let's just say a short prayer."

"Okay," said Jonathan shyly. His dad's request reminded Jonathan of how serious this situation was — and of how much his dad had changed.

"Dear Father, we come to You now, understanding that You know all things and that all things are in Your hands. We thank You for the shelter You've provided and ask You to keep us safe until someone finds us. In the name of Jesus, Amen."

"Amen," said Jonathan.

The two sat next to the comforting warmth of the fire, slightly back from the cave opening. Soon the musty smell of the cave was overpowered by smoke from the warm fire. The heat felt good on their damp bodies. Shadows made by the flickering flames danced on the walls around them.

Kendall sat back against the cave wall, relaxing for the first time in hours. He looked at Jonathan with fatherly pride, seeing how he took everything in stride. Kendall sighed with contentment. He realized how fortunate he was to have a good son. He understood that this was mainly due to Angela, his wife. Through every problem they'd encountered, he'd seen in Angela the same joy for life that had first attracted him to her. Though this last year had been hard, she was still as beautiful as ever. He pictured her now — tall and slim with chin-length, light blonde hair. He loved the sparkle in her eyes and how they changed from blue to green depending on what she was wearing. She was a true friend.

*Dear Lord, please reassure Angela that we're safe, and let her get help for us. You know how much I love her, Lord.* Kendall prayed quietly, his eyes misting over.

Jonathan watched his dad relax and felt the tension in his own young body decrease. Basking in the cozy warmth of the fire and watching the hypnotic shadows playing on the cave wall, a feeling of contentment crept over him. He realized he'd enjoyed this adventure so far. "It's a good thing we found wood in here," he said, making conversation.

"That's true. I guess God's watching over us."

"But what about the smoke, won't it get us?"

"Nope. See how it's following the incline of the cave ceiling right out the mouth of the cave?" Kendall explained.

"Yeah. This place is like that verse in Psalms that talks about the Lord being a shelter in the storm," said Jonathan.

"Yep. That's what this place is until help comes," agreed Kendall.

"Hello down there!" Jim's voice echoed from the mouth of the cave.

"Hello!" Kendall answered, startled. "We're down here!"

Jim's voice echoed down from the darkness above, competing with the sound of the storm. "Hey, is everyone okay? I saw the abandoned truck down in the ravine."

"We're fine. It didn't take you guys long to find us!" Kendall yelled up through the mouth of the cave.

"Find you? Oh no, we were trying to run from the storm but couldn't get past the fallen tree. Do you think this place may be high enough to wait out the storm?"

"That's what we're hoping . . . praying for!" Kendall yelled.

Just then Jonathan gasped as the dog who had cornered him peered down into the hole. "Watch out! There's a wild dog behind you!"

"Dog?" Jim spun around. Standing there, soaking wet, was Shadow. "Shadow? You made it!" Jim shouted, hugging the dog tightly.

"That's your dog?" exclaimed Jonathan.

"Yes, I thought I'd lost him," Jim explained. "I'm here with my wife and daughter. Is there room down there for us?"

"Yes, but watch out. It's a steep incline," said Kendall.

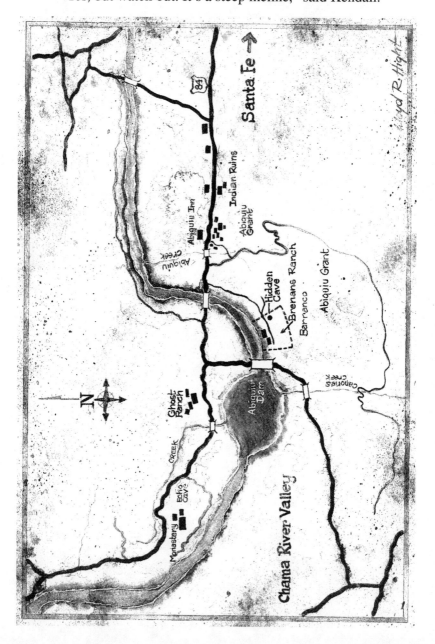

# 2

# Deep into the Cave

*O*utside the cave, it was still storming. Inside, five damp strangers and one wet dog huddled near the cozy fire to dry out. The flickering flames provided just enough light to make out their faces.

Jonathan had retreated farther back into the cave, away from the dog.

"I can't believe you made it, boy!" said Jim, petting Shadow.

"Jonathan, what are you doing back there?" asked Kendall.

"I'm trying to get away from that wild dog!" Jonathan yelled, backing farther into the cave.

"You mean Shadow here?" asked Jim.

"Yes! That dog tried to bite me when I was on my way to the cave. It's vicious!"

Kendall looked at the wiggling, happy dog Jessie was now hugging. "Are you sure it was this dog, Jonathan?"

"Positive. He was scary. He was gonna bite me."

They all looked at the dog that appeared quite innocent.

"So, how'd you get away from him?" asked Kendall.

"I barked back at him."

Everyone laughed.

"He's just a big puppy," said Jessie. "Maybe he just needed to meet you. What's your name?"

"I'm Jonathan Park and this is my dad."

"Yes, I'm Dr. Kendall Park."

"Well, Jonathan and Dr. Park, this is Shadow," said Jessie.

Jonathan took a cautious step closer to the dog, and Shadow sniffed his hand.

"See, he's not so bad," said Jessie.

"Not now," muttered Jonathan, while Shadow wagged his tail and looked up at him.

"What a cozy fire!" said Martha.

"It sure is. Someone's watching over us. Thanks for letting us share your cave," Jim said as he warmed his hands by the fire. "You mentioned prayer, are you a prayin' man?"

"Well, for most of my life, no," explained Kendall as the shadows from the fire danced on his face. "But I am now. And you?"

"Wholeheartedly. I was raised a farmer and so was my father. And you can't grow crops and go through storms without seein' the hand of God, right, Martha?"

"That's for sure. We've seen God work some mighty miracles. And it looks like He's got His work cut out for Him tonight."

"I'll say! I'm Jim Brenan. This is my wife, Martha, and daughter Jessica — who looks to be just about the same age as your son."

"Daaad," Jessica said, embarrassed. Then she added, "Most people call me Jessie for short."

Jim continued, "She's ten. We also have a four-year-old named Ryan. Fortunately, he's staying with Grandma tonight. We were trying to escape the flood. Thought we could skirt around our property until we made it to safety. . . . 'til the tree."

"Is this your cave?" asked Kendall.

"Your cave?" Jonathan blurted out, surprised.

"Technically, I guess, yes. That's probably why our dog Shadow was being so territorial. I'm sorry that he scared you. He's never bitten anyone, but he can look ferocious."

"I bet he would've bitten me if I hadn't scared him," said Jonathan.

"Wow! I never knew we had a cave before!" exclaimed Jessie.

"Neither did I," said Jim.

"From the outside I would have never guessed it was more than a little hole, but once you get through that tunnel, it's huge,"

Martha exclaimed, as she looked upward.

"It's big enough to be a tourist attraction," Kendall pointed out.

"Mom, Dad, can Jonathan and I take Shadow and look around just a little bit?" Jessie asked with her most convincing voice.

Martha began to shake her head, "It's awfully dark. . . ."

"Jonathan, remember you need to stay close in case help arrives," warned Kendall.

Martha paused and in a cautious tone said, "Well, as long as you stay where you can hear us."

"Great, Mom. We'll be just around the corner," Jessie said excitely.

"C'mon, Shadow." Shadow jumped up and wagged his tail.

"Well, aren't you coming, Jonathan?" asked Jessie.

Shadow looked at him playfully, hunched down and barked.

"Dad, she's just a girl. She'll need someone to go with her besides that dog. Can I?"

"Okay," said Kendall.

"Thanks, but I don't need a bodyguard. Besides, I have Shadow," said Jessie.

"Oh, right," said Jonathan sarcastically. "Well, let's go then, unless you're having second thoughts. Its pretty dark."

"Follow me!" said Jessie. The two started down the dark tunnel with flashlights in hand and Jessie in the lead. Shadow was right on her heals, panting happily.

"She's never at a loss for words, that one, and she loves adventure," said Jim, watching Jessie go.

"Then she and Jonathan will get along great — if he can get past the fact that she's a girl. He and his older sister go round and round," remarked Kendall. "We've had a tough year, and he's not sure who to trust. He could use a good friend about now."

"Well, Jessie's not your average girl," said Martha. "She's too full of life for the girls around here. It'd be nice for her to have a friend, too."

Jim asked, "So, what brought you two this way?"

"Well, it's a long story. . . ." Kendall began.

Jessie and Jonathan continued deeper into the cave. By now it had narrowed to about ten feet across. Their flashlights glided along the strange contour of the cave wall. Jonathan stopped to feel the rough, brown texture, running his hand over splotches of orange and red. "Whoa, isn't this amazing?"

Long, cone-shaped rocks hung down from the ceiling and jutted up from the floor. "It's beautiful!! Look at those stalagmites and stalactites," said Jessie. "They're so tall! This one's as tall as me!"

Shadow tagged along behind them, stopping to sniff the sides of the cave and the stalagmites scattered across the floor. His nose took in the musty smells of the cave and the animals living there.

"It's hard to believe that little drops of mineral water falling from the ceiling formed them. Day in and day out, drip, drip. Then voila! They form these strange rock formations. Look, when I shine my flashlight just right, don't they look like gigantic teeth. Roar," she pretended.

"Why do girls always have to pretend everything? C'mon. What I'm looking for is along the walls," Jonathan said, running his hand across the rough sides. "How do you know so much about stalagmites anyway?" asked Jonathan distractedly.

"I read," she said sarcastically. "What are you looking for?"

"Oh, nothing you'd be interested in."

"Try me," said Jessie, losing patience.

"Well, my dad said that ocean fossils are sometimes found in cave walls."

"Do you think there could be dinosaur fossils in here?" Jessie asked, shuddering with excitement at the idea.

"Not likely! I've never heard of a dinosaur fossil being found in a cave. But my dad was telling me about how in 1947 they found tons of dinosaurs just north of here."

"At Ghost Ranch! I've heard of that," Jessie exclaimed.

"Yeah they found about 1,000 Coelophysis, but they think there's a lot more. We were on our way there when we got stuck here," said Jonathan.

"Ce-lo-fike-us dinosaurs?" Jessie struggled to repeat the strange term.

"Coelophysis," Jonathan corrected.

"All I remember is that they weren't very big," said Jessie.

"Yeah, but they were still pretty scary," said Jonathan defensively. "They had slender bodies and long, narrow heads. They had lots of sharp teeth, powerful rear legs, and hollow bones that were made for speed!"

"Are those the kinds of things you and your dad were looking for?"

"Yeah, well, any kind of dino. That's kind of what we. . . uh, my dad, does now for a living. He's a freelance writer for scientific magazines. He does research by looking for dinosaur fossils and other stuff."

"It's nice to know you do something other than complain about girls. Isn't it fun going all kinds of places?"

"Yeaaah, it's fun . . ." Jonathan said unenthusiastically, kicking at the hard floor of the cave.

"But . . ." prompted Jessie.

"But now I never get to see my friends, if you can call them that. I was real close to them before, but then everything changed. It's like one day we were best friends and the next day, we weren't. And now when I see them it's weird."

"What changed?"

"It's a long story."

"Well, don't feel too bad — my best friend is . . . was, a cow."

"A cow?" Jonathan asked in disbelief.

"Yeah, her name was Molly B. The 'B' stood for Brenan. I think we lost her in the flood," Jessie said feeling sad. "We live way out on the farm, and I guess I'm kind of a tomboy, so I don't have much in common with most girls. I mean, I still like dolls and stuff, but compared to this?"

"What about Shadow here? He looks like good company."

"I guess so. He's always kind of been my dad's dog. We call him Shadow because when he was little, all he did was follow my dad everywhere he went. Where is he anyway?"

Jonathan directed his light to the left, revealing an opening in the rock side. "I think he went into that tunnel. Let's see where it goes."

"Sure," said Jessie, peeking into the opening.

"Follow me," Jonathan said with a twinge of admiration for this girl who actually liked dinosaurs. Of course, she also considered a cow her best friend. He wasn't quite sure what to think about that.

"So how long have you been looking for fossils?" Jessie asked.

"Just since last year. My dad used to work for a museum. He's a paleontologist. He put together some of the biggest dinosaurs. Some you've probably heard about."

"Really?" asked Jessie, curious.

"Yeah! He was very important. But the more he studied fossils and dinosaurs, the more he started realizing they weren't as old as everyone said — you know, 65 million years."

"Course not. The Bible mentions them," Jessie said.

"Well, back then my dad didn't want anything to do with the Bible. But the evidence also seemed to show that most of the dinosaurs were killed by lots of water."

"He found evidence that they were killed by a flood? Where?" Jessie questioned.

"In rocks, in the fossils, everything. It's just like those guys who found those fossils at Ghost Ranch. They realized that all of those dinosaurs had been killed at the same time by a great amount of water."

"Noah's flood?" asked Jessie.

"Exactly, but the guys who found them believe in evolution, so they don't have a good explanation for what happened. They say a lot of water killed them, but they don't believe in Noah's flood. But, from what my dad says, the fossils fit perfectly with the flood of the Bible. That's why we were going to investigate."

"Shadow?" Jessie called, breaking ahead to investigate. Then she screamed.

"What's wrong?" Jonathan asked.

"Jonathan, there's a face in that rock!" cried Jessie. There in her flashlight's path was a stalagmite. About three-quarters of the way up was a little face.

"You don't have to scream about it! It's not alive," He scoffed, moving closer to the stalagmite. "Wow, it's a bat fossil! It got caught in this stalagmite!"

"It just startled me. How can you tell it's a bat fossil?" Jessie asked as they walked closer to it.

Jonathan rubbed his hand along the formation as he explained. "Look, here's its head. And its wings are drooping down on the sides . . . right here."

"The stalagmite looks like melted wax that trapped the poor little guy," said Jessie. "How did it get stuck in the middle like this?"

"Well, I bet the stalagmite just kept growing," guessed Jonathan.

"Are you guys okay?" yelled Martha from the mouth of the cave. "I thought I heard a scream."

"We're fine!" Jessie yelled, her voice echoing back through the cave to the others.

Martha breathed a small sigh of relief that the kids were okay, and then turned her attention again to Kendall as he told his story.

"Kendall, do you mean to tell me that you think that man and dinosaurs lived together?" Jim asked.

"If, on day six in Genesis, God really created man and all of the land-dwelling animals together, then man and dinosaurs had to live together, right?" The other two nodded in agreement. Kendall reached over and placed another piece of wood on the fire. Embers sparked and flew into the air, making the three step back for a moment. Then as the log began to burn, they took their previous places around the fire. Kendall continued, "For the last few years I've been studying different accounts of dragons. Did you realize that many civilizations have passed down dragon legends through the centuries?"

"That's interesting," commented Jim.

Kendall continued, "What if these legends weren't just stories, but the actual accounts of real creatures. Just think about it — the word dinosaur wasn't invented until the 1800s. What if humans actually did see dinosaurs in the past but called them dragons? That would explain the dragon legends."

"That's true — the idea of dragons has always been around," Martha pointed out.

"Yes, as a matter of fact, in the British Museum in London, there's a very old book titled *The Anglo-Saxon Chronicles*. In this book are several stories of humans who saw dragons. There are so many similar accounts that are recorded in a historical manner, it makes you wonder if they can all be myths. Did you know the Bible also mentions dragons?"

"It does?" asked Jim in disbelief.

"Yes," Kendall continued. "The Hebrew word for dragon is *tannim*.. And it's used in the Old Testament over 20 times."

"I didn't realize that," said Martha. "However, I did know

that in Job, chapters 40 and 41, there are creatures that sound like dinosaurs. What are they, behemoth and leviathan?"

"That's right," affirmed Kendall. "And although I haven't had a chance to personally view them, there have been reports of ancient stone drawings that appear to look remarkably similar to dinosaurs. They've been found in Arizona at Havasupai Canyon and in Utah at Natural Bridges National Park. Others have been found in the Nazca desert plains of Peru. Although we cannot be sure what these drawings actually mean, they are interesting."

Both Martha and Jim leaned forward, wrapped up in Kendall's story. "That's fascinating," Jim commented, resting his chin in his hands.

"Yes. Dinosaur fossils hadn't yet been found. So how could Indians have drawn these creatures unless they'd seen them? I learned these things while I was still an evolutionist. That's when I began to wonder if dinosaurs had really lived millions of years ago. But that was just the beginning. I started finding dinosaurs buried in heaps by what seemed to be a great water catastrophe. So I started sharing this new information with some of my colleagues. I figured they'd be excited. . . ."

"Uh-oh. Bet they weren't," Martha interrupted.

"You've got that right!" Kendall exclaimed. "You know, people, even scientists, don't always care about what's true — only what's popular."

Farther back in the cave, Jonathan and Jessie were deciding what to do about the bat fossil.

"Let's go show them what we found!" Jessie said excitedly, heading back to the cave opening.

"Wait," said Jonathan grabbing her arm. "Just calm down a minute. If we tell them now, then we'll have to go back. Let's show them after we look around a little more."

"Okay," she said shaking her arm free from Jonathan. "But you don't have to be so grouchy about it."

"Sor-ry," said Jonathan without a hint of a real apology in his voice.

"Some people," Jessie mumbled, retreating farther into the cave. "Come on, Shadow."

Shadow turned back to Jonathan and whined as if inviting him to come.

Feeling a bit guilty, Jonathan tagged along behind her. They both stopped short at a large underground pool of water. Drips fell downward from stalactites, making big circles in the multi-colored pool below.

"Wow!" said Jessie.

Shadow started to drink from the pool. "Stop it, Shadow!" ordered Jessie, holding him back. "You don't want to end up in there." Shadow wanted a drink so badly she really had to restrain him. "Sit, boy, sit," said Jessie.

Obediently, Shadow sat down.

"So, I believe you were starting to tell me your long story," Jessie said.

"I don't know why I'm telling you all this."

"Probably 'cause there's no one else to tell and you know you'll probably never see me again. Anyway, have a seat next to this pond and tell me all about it."

Jonathan sat down, once again lost in thought. "When my dad started finding this stuff, he started to look everywhere for other people who realized that the evidence wasn't fitting with the evolutionary story. And the only other places he found were organizations and people who believed in a Creator."

"That's us," Jessie said with a smile in her voice.

Jonathan's face became a little more serious: "Then one day it happened. . . ."

"What?"

"I remember I was helping Mom set the table. My best friend Mark was over for dinner," Jonathan said, thinking back to the scene in his mind. He pictured the house. It had been the only home he had ever known. It was a big, four-bedroom house, with a study and a den and dark wood furniture that looked solid and secure. Usually it was quiet and warm. But on that night it was different. Colder. The picture was clear in his mind. He could hear the doorbell ringing and ringing. The cave faded away and Jonathan was lost in his memory of that evening. Jonathan saw his mother, Angela, open the door to find Kendall with his arms full of boxes. He could hear her as she asked, "Kendall? What happened?"

"I've been fired," Kendall said, with anger rising in his voice.

"Fired?" breathed Angela. "Why? What reason did they give you?"

Kendall stomped toward the den with boxes piled high. "They said that my recent conclusions failed to uphold the most current scientific research. Meaning I didn't classify them using their system which automatically makes things millions of years old. Because I didn't use their time frame, they said my conclusions were unreliable. They called me a loose cannon in the scientific field." A box fell to the ground. "Augh!" he said, leaving it and other items that had fallen on his way to the den.

"I . . . I'm sorry, Kendall." Angela was at a loss for words. "Here, let me help you with that stuff," she said, trying to grab the top box.

Kendall pulled away. "No, I'm fine. I've got it! I'm just taking it to my new office in the den," he said, his voice trailing off as he stomped to the next room.

"Kendall," Angela said, trying to calm him as she followed picking up the stray items. "I know this comes as a big blow. But somehow it's gonna be okay," she said unconvincingly.

"Oh, sure it will," he said brushing her away. "It's only the end to everything we've worked for all these years. My reputation, our future!" Kendall spit out the words bitterly as he dropped the boxes on his desk.

"Lower your voice," Angela whispered, eyeing Jonathan and Mark who were standing frozen in the doorway of the den. "Jonathan, can you and Mark finish setting the table?" Angela asked, her eyes misting over. She felt as if the whole family was teetering on the edge of a cliff, and it was up to her to save them — only she couldn't.

Jonathan came face to face with Mark in the dining room. "So your dad got fired, huh?"

"Yeah, just because he wasn't sure that dinosaurs lived millions of years ago," said Jonathan.

"Well, my dad knows they did!" Mark taunted.

"Well, my dad knows more about dinosaurs than your dad, so maybe mine's right!"

"My dad says your dad is nuts!"

"My dad is not crazy," protested Jonathan, as he shoved Mark.

"Well, then, maybe you're not playin' with a full deck, either. I guess the guys were right about you."

"What do you mean?"

"Don't you know? The whole gang thinks your family's weird. Nobody wants to be your friend anymore except for me, and now I'm leaving, too!" Mark said. Then he crossed over to the door to leave.

"Mark! Wait!" shouted Jonathan as Mark left, shutting the door behind him. Jonathan felt cold and alone. Mark had been his best friend ever since he could remember. Jonathan had noticed that lately the rest of the gang had treated him a little differently, and wondered if they'd talked about him behind his back. He'd always counted on the fact that Mark would stand up for him . . . until now.

Angela met Jonathan in the doorway. He was crying. "Where's Mark?" she asked.

"He left. He said Dad was crazy. Mom, what are we going to do?" Jonathan's safe world seemed to be crumbling before his very eyes.

"I don't know, but it's gonna be okay," said Angela hugging Jonathan. After a moment she stood up, cupped Jonathan's face in her hands, and looked him squarely in the eyes. "Your father stuck to the truth and that's on our side."

"What about our life here? My friends?" Jonathan said, pulling away.

"Jonathan, I know you want friends, but you can't keep friends if it means leaving the truth behind. Do you understand what I mean by that?"

"Yeah, you mean I can't pretend I believe something that's wrong, just to keep my friends."

"That's right! Any friend or job worth having won't ignore the truth. Remember that."

"Truth!" Kendall bellowed sarcastically from the den. "Yeah, follow your old dad's example. Look where it got him!"

"Kendall!" Angela reproved. "You know you don't mean that!" Angela turned back to reassure her son. "Your father is just upset right now, Jonathan. You know how important the truth is to him. Now, go ahead and set the table." Then all at once she was filled with the peace of God. It was a feeling she had almost forgotten after having spent so many years ignoring Him. She knew at once that it was going to be okay. She realized that Kendall's stand for truth was actually a step closer to finding the God she had at one time known so closely. In a whisper she said, "It's okay, son, I know that God has everything under control."

"It's time he understood how the world works, Angela," Kendall shouted, poking his head out the door of the den. "Jonathan, the truth is highly overrated!"

"We'll be back in a minute, Jonathan." Angela turned quickly and closed the door to the den behind her.

"I couldn't hear the rest of the conversation, but from what I did hear, I could tell that my dad was really mad," Jonathan said to Jessie. "When we finally had dinner, it was real quiet. Later, I heard my older sister Katie crying in her room."

"So what did you guys do?" asked Jessie.

"Well, Dad just wanted to get out of there, so we sold our home and went to live with my grandfather in Santa Fe for a while. We go there when we're not out on the road." Jonathan pictured his grandpa Benjamin's house on that first day they moved back. He remembered pulling up to the pinewood home nearly hidden by shrubs. He could still smell the chimney smoke mixed with glue fumes from his grandfather's latest project. His grandpa always had some invention half-built in the garage. The memory was so vivid that his mind traveled back in time.

"It's great to have you back," said Benjamin Park, giving Kendall a warm hug.

"Thanks, Dad. Sorry to thrust myself and the family on you like this." His voice was husky, on the edge of tears.

"Hey," Grandpa Benjamin reproved, "that's not the way I think of it at all. To tell you the truth, I'm looking forward to the company. These last few years since Ruth died have been lonely. Of course, I've got my friends and inventions, but they don't match up to family."

"I'm not sure I'm very good company right now," confessed Kendall, dropping his bags in the hallway. "There's just so much to think about. I'm so confused right now I don't know what's true."

"Oh, I think you knew the truth back there when you were telling them what you found. I'm proud of you for standing up for it. As far as being confused, sometimes the answer to what lies ahead can be found by going back to where you began. And that's right here. I know you haven't put much stock in the Lord, but He hasn't forgotten you. And as far as truth goes, in John 14:6 Jesus says, 'I am the way, the truth and the life. . . .' I think that may be a good place to start looking for that truth you've misplaced," said Benjamin.

"Well, I've tried to find the truth on my own, and so far I've just made a mess of things. Maybe you're right, Dad. Just maybe . . ." Kendall faded off into thought.

"And that's what he did," said Jonathan. "He stayed up late, just thinking and reading, night after night. He read through the whole Bible, I think," Jonathan said, looking at Jessie in the beam of his flashlight.

"Wow."

"And that's when he finally believed in the whole thing."

"What?"

"The whole Bible, especially the story in Genesis where God created everything."

"Some Christians don't even believe that," Jessie said sadly.

"You're right. A lot of Christians believe in Jesus, but they don't believe that God created the earth like it says in Genesis. But finally, it all made sense to my dad," Jonathan explained. "C'mon. Let's see what's up here."

"And what about you?" asked Jessie as the two began walking again. Neither of them had stopped to think about the fact that they had traveled farther than their parents would have wanted them to go.

"Well, it was hard to understand everything. I mean, I always kind of knew I didn't come from apes and stuff. But I didn't know what Jesus dying on a cross had to do with me." Jonathan paused. "But then I realized that if God had really made us, then He was in charge. And then when I saw such a big change in my dad — I wanted what he had. So I talked to my mom and she told me that since God had made me, I needed to let Him be the boss of my life. And in His Word, God said that because we all do wrong things, that we deserved to be punished. That's why Jesus died on the cross, to take the punishment I deserved."

"The boss? You mean accept Jesus as Lord?"

"Yeah, you know, Jesus gets to be the one in control. So I asked the Lord to forgive me for the bad things I've thought and done, and told Him He could call the shots. Mom also told me it wasn't always going to be easy. She was right about that. My friends thought I was loony."

"Because you're a Christian?"

"Yeah, and because of the creation stuff. Most of their parents are scientists."

"Like Mark?"

"Yeah, and all my friends," Jonathan said in a gloomy tone.

"I'm sorry. So what happened after that?"

"We bought this motor home and now my dad does research and writes articles for science magazines. Lots of the magazines won't take his stuff because of what happened, but some do. We use that money plus the cash left from the house we sold to live."

"Sounds like a big change." As Jessie talked, they both noticed that her voice was echoing much more.

"Wow! Look at this huge room. You could park a couple of buses in here," Jonathan said, sweeping his light along rock walls that reached majestically up at least three stories. It was about 80 feet from one wall to the next. Stalactites hung from the ceiling like rock icicles. Dome-shaped stalagmites lined the entrance of the room as if they were soldiers guarding a castle. To Jonathan and Jessie they looked like huge stacked mushrooms. As the two kids and Shadow walked into the room, their flashlights glided over colorful rock spires climbing to the ceiling. At the front of the room, the stalagmites stood in rows, looking like the chimes on a huge pipe organ. The whole room looked as if it was made from melting wax.

Jessie exclaimed, "Wow, this looks like a big church cathedral, only underground! Hello!" her voice echoed.

# 3
# The Secret Fossil

Martha, Jim, and Kendall were now completely dry and wondering where their children were.

"They've been gone a long time. I think we'd better go find them," said Martha.

Jim and Kendall both agreed, and the three set out to find the kids.

Further back in the cave, Shadow was whining and barking at the wall on one side of the cathedral.

"What's in there, boy?" asked Jessie pressing her ear against the side of the cave. "Hey, listen," she said, banging on the wall. "It sounds hollow!"

"Maybe there's another room . . ." Jonathan started to say, but he was interrupted by a rustling and shrieking sound that was getting closer and closer!

Jessie let out a scream, "Ahhhhhhhhh!"

"Bats!" Jonathan cried out. Suddenly the air was alive with rustling wings circling around them. The sounds of flapping and screeching filled the cave. The bats were so thick it seemed as if there was no air left to breathe. Jonathan and Jessie couldn't see each other through the swarm!

Shadow was barking and chasing the bats, adding to the confusion. His barks echoed loudly off the cave walls.

"Jonathan, help!"

"Jessie, it's okay! Don't run!" Jonathan yelled, beating at them with his flashlight.

But Jonathan was too late. In order to get away from the bats, Jessie was running wildly in the blackness of the room. Suddenly, in the beam of his flashlight, Jonathan thought he saw the cave floor come to an end. "Jessie, stop! There's a big drop-off!"

Just then Jessie lost her footing and toppled over the edge. "Jonathan!" she screamed.

"Jessie!" Jonathan cried out, running to the edge and looking into the darkness.

There was silence except the sound of rocks hitting the ledge on the way down. All of the bats were gone, vanishing as quickly as they appeared. There was a brief moment of eerie silence. Jonathan wondered for a split second where the bats had gone. "Jessie?"

"Jonathan . . ." came the trembling voice from somewhere below.

"I told you not to run!" Jonathan scolded, trying to see her. He was relieved she was still alive.

"Jonathan, can we please not argue right now?"

Shadow looked around questioningly, then ran to an opening past the cathedral. He scratched and barked, looking for the bats, not realizing that Jessie had gone over the edge.

"Jessie, I can't see you! Where are you?" Jonathan asked with intensity. He shined his light down the deep chasm, unable to see either Jessie or the bottom of the cave. Instinctively he stepped back as rocks tumbled over the edge, falling into silence.

"Wherever you are, hold on tight!" said Jonathan.

"Jonathan, the strap on the back of my overalls is caught on something . . . it's the only thing holding me!" A beam of bright light was shooting up from the ledge below. It was Jessie's flashlight. Jonathan quickly ran and looked down to where the light was coming from.

"Jessie?" Jonathan said, looking over the edge.

"Jonathan." Jessie's fear-filled voice came from below. "The strap on my overalls is starting to tear. Give me your hand!"

Shadow turned around to see what was going on and whined, edging closer to the cliff.

Jonathan could hear the deadly sound of ripping cloth. He looked down, but the beam of light shined too brightly in his face.

"Jessie, your flashlight is blinding me!"

"Jonathan, I can't help it! I dropped it!" Jessie said as the cloth ripped a little more. "Hurry, give me your hand!"

"Jessie, I can't see you!"

"Oh, Jonathan, I don't want to fall!" she wailed.

Jonathan yelled with all of his might, "Dad, Heelllp!" His plea for help echoed throughout the cave, reaching the ears of Kendall, Martha, and Jim.

Meanwhile, in a dark hotel room in Santa Fe, the blue glow of the television flashed on three middle-aged men sitting across from the screen.

On the couch, Marvin Potts, a short, heavy-set, balding man flipped through the channels. He paused on the cartoon channel. "Heh, heh, heh!"

"Marvin, give me that remote!" Simon ordered, grabbing it out of his hand. Simon Addleman was Marvin's opposite — tall and slim, with a full head of dark hair. While Marvin was simple-minded and rough, Simon was clever and cultured. From his recliner, Simon gave Marvin a menacing look.

"What?" questioned Marvin under the heat of Simon's stare.

"Imbeciles!" Simon said to himself. Simon looked with contempt at both of his cohorts. He knew he intimidated the other two and used that knowledge to his advantage. Vinnie was a well-built Italian man of few words. Simon didn't mind Vinnie alone, but he came as a package deal with his cousin Marvin.

"Just be quiet," Vinnie whispered to Marvin.

Vinnie's constant effort to control Marvin was almost as annoying as Marvin's whining. Neither of the motley pair seemed to be able to think for themselves, which, Simon realized, was fortunate for him. Turning his attention toward the TV, Simon consoled himself with the fact that they were cheap workers and they came in handy for the scare tactics he often used on his victims. *Besides*, he thought, *sometimes one has to lower one's standards to get the job done.*

As Simon pushed the buttons, the television changed to channel seven. The evening news filled the screen. "Gentlemen, to stay on the cutting edge, we need to know what's going on in this world."

"But, boss, I hate the news! It's just so depressin'. Too many criminal types out there," whined Marvin.

"Yes, there is a lot of competition, but if we're going to keep up with them. . . ." Simon stopped in mid-sentence to focus on the television. On the screen was a graphic that said "Local Flood Watch."

The newscaster began the story. "While Santa Fe has been fighting its own battles during the severe storms, other areas in the county have been devastated. Joan Wong joins us live with the story. Joan. . . ."

"Boss, news about the flood! Oh, wow, look at that barn just floatin' like a boat," Marvin interrupted the broadcast.

"Shhhhh!" Both Vinnie and Simon commanded.

The picture on the screen changed to the live broadcast from Abiquiu Dam. "Thanks, Ted," said Joan. It was a close-up of the reporter. "Due to extreme rainfall, the U.S. Army Corps of Engineers has been letting massive amounts of water over Abiquiu Dam. Unfortunately, this has caused severe flooding for the ranches below the reservoir. As you can see behind me, these farms have been hit the hardest. Emergency teams are working hard to evacuate the families that live here. Unfortunately, this particular property has received the most damage, yet rescue teams have not located the Brenan family that lives there. Rescue teams are currently searching the area."

"The Brenan family, aye? If they're still alive, we just may have to pay them a visit," stated Simon.

"What for, boss?" asked Vinnie.

"Well, Vinnie, look at their property — it's ruined. Their entire farm, along with their pathetic little future, has been ruined. If they're still around, I'll bet they'll sell cheap. This is where an opportunist like myself can make a deal."

"How so, boss?" asked Marvin.

"Well, it may look bad, but it's never so bad as it seems. The land I get for pennies, I can make look really good to someone else, and sell at quite a profit. Oh, how I love a natural disaster!"

The TV screen went black as Simon hit the power button. "Gentleman, I think we're in business!"

Deep in the cave, Jonathan had to keep his mind from spinning as he tried to think of what to do to save Jessie. Then he remembered that his dad had told him to bring a rope. He hadn't needed it, so it was still in his pack.

"Jonathan, hurry! My strap is breaking!" pleaded Jessie.

"I'm working on it," he said, unzipping his pack. He tied a round loop in the rope and lowered it down. "Can you see the rope?" Jonathan questioned.

"No!"

"Look for it Jessie!"

"I'm looking," she said, stressing each word.

"Here, Shadow," Jonathan called. Shadow was immediately by his side.

"Does your dog play tug of war?"

"Yes, but what does that have to do with anything?"

"When the rope gets to you grab it and tie it around you." Jonathan felt a tug on the rope and then waited for what seemed like hours, though it was only a couple of minutes, to hear from Jessie.

"Okay, it's around me."

Jonathan put the rope in Shadow's mouth. "Here, boy," he said, tugging on the rope. Shadow's jaws clenched and he backed away and growled. "That's right, just like tug of war!" Just then Jessie's strap ripped loudly.

"Jonathan!" Jessie yelled. Jonathan felt the rope tighten. The sound of rocks toppling off the ledge echoed through the room.

"Gotcha!" Jonathan cried in victory as Jessie hung tightly to the rope. "Now, let's pull, Shadow."

"Hurry!" screamed Jessie.

"Don't look down, Jessie. We got you." Inch by inch, Jonathan and Shadow pulled Jessie up over the edge to safety.

"Jessica! Jonathan!" called Mrs. Brenan from farther down the cave.

"Jessie!" Jim called out.

Martha came huffing and puffing down the tunnel, followed closely by Jim and Kendall. "I thought I heard a yell."

"Yeah . . . there were these bats. That's why Jessie, uh, fell," said Jonathan cautiously.

Martha noticed Jessie's tousled hair and dangling overall strap. "Fell?" said Martha in horror. "Did you hurt yourself?"

"Wow, look at this chamber!" said Kendall.

"It's beautiful!" exclaimed Jim.

"Look at this — this pit your daughter almost fell into!" yelled Martha, shining her flashlight over the edge.

"The bat!" Jessie interrupted, quickly changing the subject. "Show your dad the bat."

"Oh yeah, Dad. We found a bat stuck in a stalagmite!"

"Where?" asked Kendall.

"Follow me," said Jonathan. He and Jessie led the group to the room where they'd found the fossilized bat.

"It's right around these stalagmites," Jessie said as she and Jonathan looked for it.

"There!" Jonathan said, pointing.

Kendall walked over to the stalagmite and began to study the formation. "Beautiful, beautiful!"

"What's beautiful about a bat in a stalagmite?" Martha asked, still trying to catch up with what was going on.

"I don't understand," Jim confessed. "Why would a bat be in a stalagmite?"

"Well, if I can re-create history here," Kendall said, "the bat was probably hanging from the ceiling when it died and fell right on top of the stalagmite. Then the minerals continued to drip from the ceiling and encased the bat while the stalagmite continued to grow."

"That's incredible, huh, Dad?" Jonathan marveled.

"Yeah, great evidence for creation!"

"How's that, Kendall?" Jim asked.

"Evolutionists believe that it takes millions of years for stalagmites to form. They believe that very slow drips of water deposit minerals that form stalagmites. But if that were true, this bat would have decayed long before the stalagmite formed around it.

So this stalagmite must be forming very fast."

"Dad, we've found the only bat-lagmite in the world!"

"No, Jonathan. Actually there was one similar to this found south of here, in Carlsbad Caverns." Kendall recounted. "There's a picture of it in a 1953 *National Geographic*, but very little has been written about it. This is great information for an article."

"Dad, shouldn't we get a picture of this one?"

"You're absolutely right, Jonathan. Can you get the camera out of my backpack?"

Jonathan tried to open the backpack and hold the flashlight at the same time. His light fell to the cave floor.

Suddenly, Shadow was crouching and growling, baring his teeth.

"Now that's the dog I remember," said Jonathan.

"What's wrong, boy?" asked Jessie, turning to see what had caught the dog's attention. She was met by a frightening sight that was too much for her already frazzled nerves to handle and she began to scream. Martha was close behind her and startled, screamed as well.

Jonathan turned to see what the commotion was about muttering, "Now I know where she gets i-" Jonathan stopped in midsentence, "Wha . . . what is that?"

"What's going on?" Jim exclaimed.

"Look! In that room right there!" Jessie yelled pointing a shaky finger at the cave wall in an adjacent room. "A dinosaur!"

"It's hideous!" gasped Martha.

The whole gang spun around just in time to see the silhouette of a large creature in the adjacent room! It looked as if it had a long neck and jagged spine.

"Nobody panic!" yelled Kendall.

Just west of the cave, a helicopter circled over the flooded area now covered in darkness. Two weary rescuers, pilot Marty Williams and co-pilot Randy Wade, looked for any evidence of people left behind.

"Over there on Highway 162 is where Mrs. Park said she last heard from her son," said Wade.

"The problem is, where is 162 now? Most of it is under water," Williams said.

As the helicopter neared, their light swept the swollen ravine. Wade looked through binoculars, but saw only the tops of trees. "I hate to say it, but I can't see anything. Let's try farther down the river,"

"Roger," said Williams.

As the helicopter turned to leave, Wade caught sight of dimly flashing yellow lights. "Wait! Turn around. I see something! Let's take a closer look."

❧❧

Inside the cave, the group stared at the strange figure on the wall.

"It's not moving," said Jim.

"That's just a shadow!" Kendall said, trying to calm everyone down.

"Arf, arf!"

"Not you, Shadow," said Jim.

"A shadow of what?" asked Martha.

"I'm not sure," Kendall answered, thinking through the possibilities. "I need to take a closer look."

"Dad, it looks like a dinosaur skull."

"It does looks like some type of skull," observed Kendall unemotionally.

"Look, it's from Jonathan's flashlight. When he dropped it, it landed so the light was shining on that thing," Jim said pointing at the shadow and walking cautiously toward it. The beam of light traveled into a nearby room. There, only a few feet from the entrance, was a skull sitting atop a group of closely formed stalagmites. The light shining on the skull had made the image of a dinosaur on the wall.

Shadow was still growling. "Look, boy, it's okay. It's not real," said Jim calming him down. Shadow whined, then wagged his tail at Jim's touch.

Jim reached the room and looked inside. As he moved to the archway, his body blocked the light, making the shadow disappear. Shining his flashlight around the room, he saw stalactites

reaching down like long fingers toward rising stalagmites. He started to step into the room but noticed for the first time that the stalagmites that held the fossil weren't on the floor, but sat on a ledge. He pointed his light downward and found that the floor dropped straight down at least 15 feet, like an elevator shaft. At the bottom, stalagmites shot up like dull spears, making the whole room look like a prickly torture chamber.

"Excuse me, Jim," said Kendall, stepping past him into the room. He was hit right away with a damp musty smell. "It's wet in here," he said.

The rest watched intently as Kendall carefully stepped around clusters of stalagmites and ducked under stalactites hanging almost 12 feet from the ceiling. He lost his balance and teetered on the edge. Rocks slid past him and crashed onto the stalagmites below. There was a collective gasp as the others waited from just outside the room.

"Whoa!" He grabbed a stalagmite to catch himself. "It's slippery in here."

"Is . . . is it a dinosaur skull?" Jessie asked, poking her head into the room.

"Well, it's some type of animal skull, to be sure," Kendall shouted back. "Actually, this does look like a dinosaur of some sort."

"Wow!" Jessie said, taking one step into the room.

"Stay out of there, Jessie!" Martha barked. "That's close enough."

"Oh, yeah," Jessie stepped back obediently, remembering her fall.

"What a find! This is the skull of a medium-size dinosaur, and it looks like a Coelophysis!" Kendall's joy rang out.

"Dad, I thought you said dinosaurs shouldn't be found in caves."

"That's true, I don't think this skull belongs here," said Kendall

"So, how'd it get here?" asked Jonathan.

"That's a . . . that's a great question," Kendall muttered to himself as he began looking around the room. As he looked, everyone else shined lights into the room, as if the answer was nearby.

Jim shined his light straight up. "Look!" he cried out. There, above Kendall, was a crack in the cave ceiling, about a foot wide. "No wonder it's wet in there."

"I think this gives me some ideas about where this fossil came from," said Kendall.

"How, Dad?"

"Well, I believe that this dinosaur was killed like the ones at Ghost Ranch and then. . . ."

"Shhh," said Martha, interrupting Kendall. "I heard something!"

"Helicopters!" Jonathan shouted. "I hear helicopters!"

"They're looking for us!" Martha cried out with relief.

"Come on, let's go!" yelled Jim.

"I can't leave now! This is one of the most amazing finds!" Kendall said.

"You guys, we're going to miss the helicopters!" Jessie reminded them.

"Dad, the helicopters are our only way out!"

"Kendall, we need to leave now. If we make it out, you have

my permission to return here anytime you'd like to retrieve the skull," Jim said forcefully.

Taking one last look at the fossil, Kendall said, "You're right! But everyone remember, we need to keep quiet about this. It'll be our secret here in this hidden cave. Let's go!"

4

# The Offer

An official New Mexico search and rescue truck pulled up to the home of Benjamin Park. Grandpa Benjamin's house was sided with natural pine, supporting an old-fashioned shake roof. Flowers spilled from window boxes, adding splashes of pink, red, and white. The landscape was overgrown with spindly clusters of Aspens and shrubs. The landmark was a rock wishing well in the middle of the yard. What made it stand out from the other homes was its disregard for the "Santa Fe style," which consisted of light brown adobe buildings with tiled roofs and log-beamed ceilings with the logs sticking out of the sides of the building. The house was a lot like Grandpa — he always had his own way of doing things.

On the inside of the vehicle sat a tired boy and his father. "Thanks for the ride, officer," Kendall said as he opened the door to the truck.

"No problem."

Angela Park came running out of the house and down the walkway.

"Honey, I'm home!" cried Kendall.

"And you're late!" joked Angela. "Oh, Kendall. I'm so glad you're okay!" Kendall swept her up into his arms. The rest of the family piled out of the house and waited through an embarrassing moment as Kendall kissed Angela. Then, with her feet on the ground she turned and pretended to scold Jonathan: "And you, Jonathan. You scared me half to death when the phone went dead." She grabbed his cheek and pinched it.

"Sorry, Mom."

"We were all a little worried, sport," said Grandpa, hugging Jonathan. "Even Katie."

"Really?" asked Jonathan incredulously.

"Well, kind of," said Katie.

"Kind of? Ha! It was Katie here who tuned into the weather channel and kept giving us updates on the flood," said Benjamin. "And just between us two, I think she was pretty worried," he said, just above a whisper.

"Ya know ya love me," said Jonathan, laying his head on Katie's shoulder. Meanwhile, he snuck his wet finger around her head.

"Yuck! Jonathan get your disgusting finger out of my ear!" Katie said pushing him away.

"Wet Willie. Haaaaa!" Jonathan said, making the victory sign and jumping up and down.

"Brothers!"

"Let's get you cleaned up, and then we want to hear all about it. C'mon," said Grandpa Benjamin.

"Sounds great to me." Kendall made his way toward the front door of Benjamin's house.

———❧———

Late morning sunshine shot down in brilliant rays, reflecting off still pools of water and drying out the flooded land. The Brenan ranch looked like a scene from a defeated battleground. Powerful flood currents had swept through the ranch a week earlier, leaving nearby fence posts leaning the same way. They sagged hopelessly, looking like soldiers returning home. Some posts had fallen into the mud, leaving barbed wire strewn nearby. Wood from the barn lay in red heaps. Lifeless grapevines lay in clumps, mixed with mud and trash that had washed in from somewhere else. Without the animals, all was silent.

A black Lincoln Continental glided up the hill toward the Brenans' house, which sat at the top of their property. The house looked in poor condition. The bottom half of the outside walls were faded and dirty from muddy currents that had scoured away at the painted siding. Curtains from a window just to the left of the front door parted as the car zoomed up the driveway.

Jim Brenan looked out the window as he heard the sound of a car coming up the drive. He watched suspiciously as three men walked up onto the front porch. Jim was already heading toward the door when the men knocked. He opened the door a crack. "Hello. Can I help you?"

"Yes, Mr. Brenan. My name is Simon Addleman, and I thought you may have some land for sale." Something in his voice bothered Jim. It was too smooth, too full of confidence.

"That's interesting since I don't have a 'For Sale' sign up anywhere," Jim replied.

"I'm just someone who keeps up with the news. I heard about the terrible flooding that you had in this area, and I'm the kind of guy that likes to help people out of a bind." Simon smiled, trying to peek inside the house.

"Yeah, he's a regular pilantropist," said Marvin with his thick Brooklyn accent.

"Shh!" Vinnie said, placing one finger over his mouth.

"Uh," Jim paused awkwardly while sizing up the strangers. "Won't you come in?"

The three men took a seat on the couch as Jim closed the door. They looked around at the country Victorian theme. The home was in perfect order, except for the ruined, musty carpet and furniture and water stains on the walls.

Shadow sat next to the easy chair and looked at them suspiciously.

"Honey, this is Mr. Simon Addleman and. . . ."

Simon completed his sentence, "Yes, these are my associates, Vincent Vicente and Marvin Potts."

"This is my wife, Martha."

"Hello, gentlemen," said Martha, eyeing the three men suspiciously. "Can I get you anything to drink? Coffee, perhaps?"

"Uh, ya got any. . . ." Marvin began.

"We'd all like coffee," interrupted Simon.

Marvin shot him an angry look.

"I'll help you in the kitchen, Martha," offered Jim. "Will you excuse me, gentlemen?"

"Shua," said Marvin, sitting back on the couch.

Jim and Martha retreated into the kitchen.

Watching them leave, Marvin whispered, "Boss, I was gonna have a soda."

"Mind your manners," said Vinnie.

Shadow kept his post near the chair and eyed them cautiously. Soon a low growl rumbled in his throat.

"Nice doggie," said Marvin.

"Rrruff! Rrruff!" barked Shadow.

"Shadow, get in here!" said Jim, calling him into the kitchen.

Shadow half-obeyed, lying right outside the kitchen door in the dining room so he could still see the men.

"That's a good boy," said Martha. "I don't mind him keeping an eye on them for us." Dishes clanked as she took down cups and saucers from the cupboard.

"Yeah, and more importantly, they can see him."

"Jim, who are those men out there? I don't like the looks of them," Martha said as she poured water into the coffeemaker.

"I don't know, Martha, but I think they probably prey on disaster victims for their land."

"Oh, that's comforting," said Martha sarcastically. "What do they do with it?"

"Who knows? I'm sure they plan to buy low and sell high. And right now this property is not worth much. It'll take more than a season to get our grapes back and we lost most of the livestock," Jim said.

"So, what are we going to tell them?" asked Martha, her voice rising a little.

"I think we just need to listen. Selling our land may be the only way we can make it. The key for right now is to stay calm and not panic. Fear is what guys like Simon count on."

"This is a good chance to practice loving my enemies," mumbled Martha under her breath as she prepared the coffee tray.

"What's takin' 'em so long in there, boss?" asked Vinnie. "I'm gettin' fidgety."

"Yah, and dat mangy dog is given' me the evil eye," said Marvin, looking at Shadow.

"Ruff!" barked Shadow in response to Marvin's look. Then he settled into a low growl.

"You know, dogs seem to be able to see into the black hearts of people. And you should be nervous. Imagine being ripped apart by those teeth," taunted Simon.

"Booosss," whined Marvin.

"It's a joke, Marvin. He's probably harmless. As far as the Brenans go, they're probably in there trying to figure us out," said Simon, calmly looking at his nails. "This room is quite quaint don't you think, aside from all of this water damage?"

Marvin joined in, "Yeah, whadda you care? You're just gonna turn it into a shoppin' mall or somethin'."

"I'm just going to sell it to the highest bidder, that's all. And after I snoop around a little I'll know just who that is. Shh! Here they come," Simon snapped.

"Sorry for the delay, uh, gentlemen," said Martha, entering the room. Jim followed carrying the tray of steaming cups.

Shadow came in behind Jim, once again sitting next to Jim's easy chair. This time the dog looked at each one as if he were ready to pounce.

"Here's your coffee," said Martha, retrieving the cups from the tray and passing them to the three. Marvin reluctantly took his cup, filling it with lots of milk and sugar.

"Thank you kindly — Martha, wasn't it?" Simon asked.

"Yes," Martha said, a bit sharply, sitting in a chair next to Jim's. She was uncomfortable being on a first-name basis with Simon.

"Hey, boy," said Simon, a little tense with Shadow's even glare. "Nice dog you have there, Mr. Brenan. Does he bite?"

"Only if he feels you're a threat to the family," Jim said in a half-joking tone, settling into his easy chair.

Simon laughed a bit nervously.

"So Mr. Addleman. . . ." began Jim.

"Simon."

"Okay . . . Simon," Jim said pointedly with an edge in his voice. "What can we do for you?"

"Like I said, Jim, I help folks like yourselves by buying their land."

"And what price would you be offering?" Jim asked.

"Well," Simon stopped, pausing to take a sip of his coffee and savor the taste. "Ahh, great coffee." All eyes were on him as he set down his coffee cup, pulled a slip of paper out of his pocket, and wrote down a number. "I was thinking of this price," Simon said, handing the paper to Jim.

"That's only a third of what this place is worth!" Jim yelled.

"Was worth, don't you mean?" Simon corrected sarcastically.

"Well, I haven't even had a chance to see the extent of the damage," Jim reacted, raising his voice.

*So much for staying calm*, Martha thought to herself.

"Look around, Jim!" said Simon.

"That's Mr. Brenan, to you," corrected Jim.

"All right, Mr. Brenan, I suggest you take a good look at what you have to sell. I see nothing left on this property but a few mangy animals, with no barn to put them in, and a house that needs new carpeting. There's no crops and I do believe you're late on your mortgage."

"How did you know that?" asked Jim.

"I know a lot, Mr. Brenan."

"Well, what you don't know is that there may be more to this land than meets the eye." Jim said, already wishing he had kept quiet.

"What are you saying? What could possibly be left?" Simon demanded.

"Never mind." Jim left it at that.

"Well, I may be your last chance to sell before the bank tosses you out on the street, and then where will your family be?" Simon hissed.

"In the Lord's hands, I guess, Mr. Addleman," Jim said pointedly.

"Oh, that sounds so nice, Mr. Brenan, but it doesn't seem like the Lord smiled too kindly on you recently, does it?" sneered Simon.

"Well, Mr. Addleman," said Martha, shooting up a quick prayer for kindness, "it may seem like that from your point of view, but from His, it makes perfect sense."

"Yes, but it's your point of view we're talking about, isn't it, Martha?" Simon hissed like a slippery snake.

Suddenly, the front door burst open. "Hi, Mom, we're done feeding the animals," said Jessie as she and Ryan walked into the living room. She stopped short when she saw Simon, Marvin, and Vinnie.

Shadow wagged his tail and nuzzled up to Jessie. "Hey, Shadow," she said, scratching him behind his ears.

Jessie's four-year-old brother, Ryan, ran into Martha's arms. "Mom, I got to feed the ducks!"

"What a lovely family you have," said Simon. "Come along, gentlemen." As he was leaving he whispered to Jim. "It would be awful to see anything bad happen to them."

Shadow looked once more at the men and growled.

"Is that a threat, Mr. Addleman?" demanded Jim.

"Oh, I rarely threaten, Mr. Brenan," hissed Simon. "Consider my offer. You won't get a better one. I'll be in touch." Simon slammed the door behind him.

Simon marched to his black Lincoln Continental, seething with anger as he waited for Marvin to let him in.

"That didn't go too well, boss," observed Marvin, shutting the door.

"Sh," Vinnie said loudly over the top of the car before getting into the driver's seat.

"Whaaat?" said Marvin settling in next to Vinnie.

Simon sat quietly for a moment in the back seat and then spoke as if thinking out loud. "Yes, Marvin's right. Mr. Brenan knows something we don't. And I bet the answer lies in the man and boy they rescued. It was in a cave, the news report said. Let's look into it, shall we?"

# 5
# The Eagle's Nest

It was a bright, beautiful morning at Grandpa Benjamin's home. The sun was shining, and the storm of the week before seemed like a faded dream. Jonathan awoke to the smell of pancakes cooking on the griddle.

"Breakfast is ready!" chirped Angela.

"Coming, Mom!" yelled Jonathan. It was the Saturday morning ritual of pancakes. As the younger brother, he knew his duty. Jonathan jumped out of bed, heading for Katie's room. Quietly he opened the door. There she was, asleep and soooo vulnerable. He ran from the door and jumped on her bed. "WAKE UP!" he yelled.

"Go away," she groaned, throwing the covers over her head. A hand popped above the blankets and blindly tried to wave him away.

"Katie, wake up, its an earthquake!" Jonathan said shaking her bed.

"Sto-op sh-a-ki-ng the be-d!" she said, her voice wavering with the motion. "Okay, Okay, I'm up!" she said, sitting straight up and glaring at him. "Now leave!" she said, pushing him off the bed.

He hit the floor running. "I'm getting the first pancake!" he said, racing out of the room.

"Hi, Mom!" Jonathan yelled, bounding down the stairs.

"Morning, Jonathan! You're looking happy this morning. Did you get Katie up?" Angela asked, putting a stack of pancakes on the table.

"Yeah, she'll be here someday. I'm doing great . . . except . . . well, I was just thinking about the Brenans and their farm," Jonathan said, helping himself to three pancakes.

"You really hit it off with Jessie — as a friend, I mean."

"She's okay, I guess . . . for a girl. But I wouldn't call her a friend. You know how girls are."

"But I'm a girl."

"I know, but you're my mom. That doesn't count. Especially because you make great pancakes." Jonathan poured syrup over his stack of pancakes and dug in.

"Besides, Jonathan, I know you don't really hate girls. That's just an excuse not to make friends."

"Girls are okay, I guess, but they're not like family."

"Honey, I'm really glad you're close to your dad and grandpa. That's wonderful, but you also need some friends your age."

"Yeah, right!" Jonathan groaned sarcastically.

"Jonathan, I know that you feel like you don't want friends, but eventually you're going to need to get over what happened in the old neighborhood."

"Yeah, but I can't, Mom," Jonathan said getting frustrated. "They made fun of me and Dad. Even my best friend Mark left, and who needs that?" He was tough on the outside, but Jonathan felt that he might cry any minute.

"Jonathan, those boys weren't true friends. When you needed them, they weren't there for you. But you still need to forgive them and be ready to go on and make new friends."

"Mom, kids my age don't understand me. When they hear how I believe, they think I'm weird," he said, chewing on a mouthful of pancake.

"You mean they think it's weird that you believe the Bible is true and that God created the earth?" asked his mom.

"Yeah."

"There are friends who'll care about you. They're out there, you know."

"Yeah, well, for now I just love hangin' around with Dad and Grandpa and you . . . and these pancakes," he said, finishing up the pancakes in front of him.

"Uh, huh," said Angela not believing a word. "What about the group of boys from Thad's house? Didn't you have fun over there?"

"I don't know. It was okay."

"Why don't you spend some time with them, and see if they are worthy of your friendship. If they are, you've gained a lot. If not, there are other kids out there. But you'll never know what kind of friends they could be unless you give 'em a chance. Why don't you go see them today!"

"Can't I just hang out with Grandpa today? He's got a new invention. . . ." Jonathan rinsed his plate and stuck it in the dishwasher.

"Jonathan, what are you going to do? Become a hermit? Go!"

"All right," he said, heading toward the stairs dejectedly.

Sitting Indian style, Thad Sherman pounded his makeshift gavel on the floor of the tree house several times before he got the other three boys' attention. Silence. Though he was shorter than the others, his take-charge style (coupled with the fact that the tree house was in his yard) made this fair, red-headed boy the undisputed leader. A breeze blew through gaps in the rickety tree house made of scrap wood and particleboard. "I think we all know why we've called this emergency meeting of the Eagle's Nest."

"Yeah, so we'd have something to do," said Mike sarcastically. Mike always had an answer or saying for everyone. Standing nearly a head taller than the others, he was both feared and respected. The boys also knew that under his tough exterior Mike was a loyal friend.

"It's to help Jonathan," Thad said, answering his own question.

"Why's he always acting like a judge?" Timmy commented under his breath. Timmy, Thad's eight-year-old brother, was tired of always taking orders from Thad.

"Because he's the big boss man!" retorted Mike.

Jonathan cleared his throat, "Well, I wondered if you guys might be able to help me figure out how to help my friends? It was a family that lost everything in the flood."

Though he was a new neighbor, Jonathan always brought exciting stories of adventure with him. His dad was famous in

their eyes because he dug up dinosaurs and was always doing something dangerous, so they were eager to help.

"Hey, guys, sorry I'm late!" Eddie yelled up to the treehouse from the ground.

Mike shouted down, "You're always late!"

Eddie shouted back, "So am I coming up, or what? Drop the ladder!"

"What's the password?" commanded Thad.

"Come on, guys, it's me. I don't need a password."

"What's the password, Eddie? And don't forget the hand motions," Mike called.

"Come on guys, it's dumb! I don't want to say it, okay?" pleaded Eddie. He secretly liked saying the password because it was a way of getting attention. Eddie was always entertaining. He was freckle-faced, curly haired — a chubby ball of fun.

"No password, no ladder, Eddie!" Mike shouted.

"Besides, you do it so well," added Thad.

Eddie finally gave in, "All right, all right. . . .

> Cock-a-doodle doo, cock-a-doodle doo,
> we'll be watching over you.
> Quackity, quackity, quack, quack, quack,
> bad guys better just turn back.
> We soar higher than all the rest,
> 'cause we're the crew from the Eagle's Nest!"

"Drop the ladder!" Thad proclaimed royally.

"So look, you guys know I was trapped in a cave, right?" Jonathan began, as Eddie huffed and puffed up the ladder.

"Yeah, yeah, we all heard about it, right guys?" said Thad.

"So, did you find any hidden treasure?" Timmy interrupted.

"Well, I promised I wouldn't say anything. But we did find a fossil. I can't tell you what kind," Jonathan answered, forgetting his fear for the moment.

Eddie had now made it up the ladder and swung his legs up into the treehouse, causing it to rock.

"Watch out, Eddie, you're shaking the treehouse!" exclaimed Mike.

"Whoa, it's a tough day at sea, sir!" joked Eddie.

"Sh, Eddie, we're trying to listen," said Timmy.

"So, what do you want us to do?" interrupted Mike.

"Well, the people we were trapped with lost all their crops and may lose their farm, and I wondered if we could help them," said Jonathan.

"Right!" Mike said sarcastically. "Like we're going to be

able to help them raise a ton of money to save the farm."

"We're gonna buy the farm because they haven't 'bought the farm' yet. Get it? Bought the farm? Ha, ha . . . ha," said Eddie. No one laughed. "Anyway. . . ."

"Eddie, this is serious," chided Thad. "Hmmm . . . this is a tough one, but there must be some way to help."

"We could sell things door-to-door?" Timmy suggested.

"We could go on TV and ask for money. Like a telethon! I'll be Jerry Lewis," Eddie said, launching into his best impression.

"No, no. That costs too much money," said Jonathan.

Suddenly there was a beeping from inside Eddie's pocket. "What's that beeping, Eddie?" asked Jonathan.

"It's my watch. I keep it in my pocket," Eddie said, as he began digging. "The hard part's finding it in here."

"Why is it beeping now?" asked Thad.

"Two o'clock — that's when it's normally time to ask my mom if I can take out the trash," Eddie explained.

Mike couldn't believe his ears. "You set your watch to remind yourself to take out the trash?"

"Since when are you so anxious to help around the house?" Thad asked suspiciously.

"See, if I take out the trash at 2:00, the ice cream man shows up about 2:10 each day," Eddie clarified, "and as long as I'm out there with the trash, I might as well get an ice cream!"

"Now, there's the Eddie we know and love," Mike chimed in.

"So, how are fossil bones made anyway?" Timmy asked out of the blue.

"Well, fossils aren't really bones." Jonathan said.

"I can't reach it, too much stuff," Eddie said as he continued to dig through his pocket.

"My Dad said that the bone is replaced by the minerals in the dirt that was around the bone and that's what makes a fossil."

"That noise is driving us crazy. If your pocket wasn't so stuffed, you'd have it turned off by now!" said a frustrated Mike.

"Hey, all this stuff's important," Eddie pointed out, ignoring the other conversation going on. "My pocket knife, a jaw breaker, a lump of pocket lint . . . firecrackers. . . ."

"Firecrackers?" Mike's interest peaked.

"Yeah, you never know when you'll need 'em! Ah, here's my watch!" Eddie turned off the alarm. "Now to set it for 9:00."

"9:00?" asked Thad.

"Of course, I always set it to 9:00 to remind me of my bed-time snack," Eddie replied as he dropped his watch back into his stuffed pocket.

"So, where do fossils come from?" Timmy persisted.

"Well, Dad said that to turn bones into fossils, it takes lots of water, mud, and pressure," Jonathan explained.

"Yeah, otherwise animal bones just rot," Thad added.

"Like that bird in Mrs. Kilenger's yard," Eddie pointed out.

"Yeah. After that cat got it, it just laid there rotting while the maggots ate it," Mike recounted with pure pleasure.

"Grroosss!" exclaimed Eddie. "That's just gross!"

"But it makes a good point," Jonathan continued. "To become a fossil, animals have to be buried deep with lots of water and mud before they rot away, and that doesn't happen very often."

"But I thought scientists have found bazillions of fossils!" Thad said.

"That's true. Dad said that it's very rare that mud and water bury living animals. That's why evolutionists say that it would have to take millions of years to make all the fossils that we find," Jonathan explained. Then, gathering his courage, he added "But that's not a very good answer."

"Really? That's all you hear in the news," challenged Mike.

"So how does it happen?" Timmy asked.

"Hey, Noah's flood!" Thad said, putting two and two together.

"Exactly! Most of them anyway," Jonathan confirmed, re-lieved.

"Right! Like that happened!" said Mike, the resident skep-tic. "Sometimes I wonder about you guys."

"Well . . ." Jonathan paused, choosing his words carefully, "there sure seems to be a lot of evidence for Noah's flood. Think about it. With all of that water, there would be lots of mud. And the Bible tells us that all the animals that didn't go in the ark drowned. And they would be covered with water and mud and lots of pressure. It would make millions of fossils!"

"Just like we find. Wow," said Eddie.

"Yeah, and my dad thinks that's a lot better explanation than the evolutionists have. He used to be an evolutionist and that explanation just didn't seem to fit with what he was seeing. He kept finding evidence that those bones were covered by a great catastrophe like a huge amount of water. That's why he wants to study fossils. He thinks it may help to show that there really was a great flood, and other things we read about in the Bible." Jonathan paused, ready for rejection.

"What do you think about that, Mike?" taunted Eddie.

"Look, guys. I'm not sayin' it didn't happen. It's just not what you hear in the news or school," said Mike defensively.

"Well, there's a lot of evidence to back up creation. I mean, my dad was one of those scientists that said the stuff you hear in school until he looked at the evidence," said Jonathan.

"All right, but what about the Brenans?" Thad said. "Remember the Brenans?"

"That's right," Jonathan joined in, breathing an inner sigh of relief. "How are we going to raise money to help them save their farm?"

"We need something to sell," suggested Eddie.

"I wish we could sell fossils," remarked Timmy.

"Fossils! Fossils!" Jonathan yelled out. "Timmy, you're a genius! Fossils are worth a ton of money! All my dad needs to do is sell a fossil to the museum. And I think I know where he can get one."

"Where?" asked Timmy.

"I can't tell you right now," said Jonathan. "But the important thing is that we did it! We found a way to keep the Brenans' farm afloat!"

"Sounds like it already was," said Eddie. The others looked at him blankly. "Afloat. Keep the ranch afloat . . . remember it was flooded? Ah, never mind!"

"We did it?" Mike said, ignoring Eddie as usual. "We actually figured out a way to raise money!"

The treehouse shook as all the boys jumped up and down giving each other high fives.

"Careful, guys. We don't want to have to raise money for this tree house next," joked Thad.

# 6
# The Scare

Vinnie and Marvin stood behind Simon, watching him tap on his computer. "Gentleman, I've accessed the Brenans' credit reports. Things are heating up quite a bit. I've had one associate pose as a government agent to turn the Brenans down for emergency assistance, and another to hound them about the mortgage payment. Ah, I do enjoy a good scam."

"Boy, boss, ya got people workin' for ya from all over," remarked Marvin. "Ain't this a lot to go through for one piece of land?"

"Mind your own business, Marvin," said Vinnie.

"Marvin! How industrious of you to ask," said Simon sarcastically.

"Tanks, boss," said Marvin, glaring at Vinnie.

"Well, Marvin, I guess some would say this is a lot to go through for one piece of land. One thing you may notice about me is that I'm a man who doesn't take 'no' for an answer. Therefore, the challenge for me, the fun, if you will, is turning that 'no' to a 'yes.' In other words, Marvin, I live for the chance to make others bend to my will. But I think we're going to make a tidy profit. I predict that soon we'll have the Brenans 'persuaded' into our little deal. If we buy their property out from under them, I think we can turn around and sell it for five times what it costs us," Simon gloated.

"Pretty smooth sailing, eh, boss?" Marvin asked.

"Well, almost. That other family bothers me. I've done a little checking, and Dr. Kendall Park seems to be a paleontologist," Simon observed.

"Yeah, uh, boss, what's a paleontologist?" asked Marvin.

"It's a person who knows all about fossils, you idiot."

"So what's wrong with him bein' one?" Vinnie asked.

"Well, what's wrong is this. If that man starts finding fossils on their property, everyone and their dog will hear about it. Suddenly, the Brenans' property will be very valuable, and they will have more offers than they'll know what to do with. And then we'll be out. We can't have them running around with evidence that there are fossils," Simon explained.

"So what are we going to do?" Vinnie asked.

"Marvin, tonight you and I are going to pay the Park family a little visit. Vinnie, you hold down the fort."

—◆—

Silverware clanked on plates as the Park family finished their evening dinner. Though the family table had been set with informal plates and placemats, and the family favorite, spaghetti, had been served, the conversation had been unusually quiet. Normally, the dinner meal sparkled with conversation about Dad's new finds, or Grandpa's latest invention, followed by reports from the Jonathan and Katie on school and homework to be finished. But tonight, everyone seemed lost in thought.

"Dad . . ." Jonathan said tentatively as he mustered courage.

"Yes, Jonathan?"

"Me and some guys were talking about the Brenans today . . ." Jonathan proceeded.

"It sure is a shame about those folks," said Grandpa.

"Yeah, I talked to Jim Brenan, and he thinks the only way out is to sell," said Kendall.

"The guys and I thought maybe you could sell a fossil. Then I was thinking, what about that fossil in their cave? Would that be enough money for the Brenans?" Jonathan suggested.

"You and the boys thought of that? That's pretty smart," Angela exclaimed.

"Jonathan, that's an excellent idea. And, as a matter of fact, I was thinking the same thing," said Kendall.

"Would that one fossil make enough money?" asked Jonathan.

"Well, Coelophysis are common. But, I think we'd be able

to make enough so the Brenans can keep their land. Besides, with Jim's permission, I want to go back and check it out."

"Kendall, do you have some museums that would be interested?" Grandpa asked.

"Yes, but before they'd be interested, they would need some pictures and a specimen. . . ."

Katie's mind wandered at all the talk about people she didn't even know. As she sat at the table, she realized she'd left her school report in the car. Mom had promised to help her put the finishing touches on it. "Mom, do you have the keys? I left my homework in the car."

"I'll go along to protect you," Jonathan said in a kidding voice.

"Oh, right!" exclaimed Katie, sarcastically. "You may come along to keep me company!"

Katie and Jonathan headed toward the front door. "We'll be back in a minute!"

Katie opened the door to a black night. Crickets chirped and the stars were bright and clear, but the moon hadn't come out. She shut the door behind them, and they stepped out into the yard. "Isn't it great to see Grandpa again?"

"Yeah, I've missed him."

Instantly the yard lighted up, "Whoa!" Katie exclaimed startled.

"What's wrong?" Jonathan asked.

"Oh, it's that motion light. It scares me every time!" Katie replied.

"It'll turn off in just a minute, as soon as we're out of its range," Jonathan said as they walked toward the car.

"Jonathan?"

"Yeah?"

"Do you see that car across the street?"

"Yeah? So?" he said.

"Have you seen either of those two guys before?"

Jonathan squinted, "No. I can barely see 'em in the dark, but they look a little creepy from here."

"Probably just waiting for friends that live around here," Katie said in a reassuring voice. "They don't look familiar."

"They look like gangsters," said Jonathan.

"Which key?" she said nervously, hunting for the right one.

"Hurry up! It's kind of spooky out here. I think it's that one," Jonathan said, grabbing a key.

"Okay!" She unlocked the car door and reached inside. "I'll just grab my binder, and we're out of here."

"Katie," Jonathan's voice said with just a little nervousness. "There's no one in their car now."

"Probably went inside a neighbor's house. Okay, I've got my . . . ." She ended her sentence with a scream. "Ahhhhhhhhh!"

Jonathan spun around just in time to see a tall man wearing a black ski mask standing right behind them! "So you're the Park kids, aye? Not a peep out of you two!" barked Simon Addleman. "Marvin, get over here!"

The motion sensor light turned off.

"Katie, run!" screamed Jonathan.

"Boss, it's one of those automatic lights," Marvin puffed, a little out of breath. He had slipped a nylon stocking over his head making his nose look even bigger and flat.

"You get the boy, I'll get the girl!" Simon commanded.

"It's too dahk!" exclaimed Marvin.

"Just look," shouted Simon. "And keep an eye on the front door." Both Simon and Marvin began to search the front yard, just out of range of the motion light.

Katie and Jonathan had hidden in the shrubs lining Grandpa's home. "Jonathan, they can't see us!" Katie whispered.

"I know, we must be blending in," Jonathan whispered back. "Our only chance is to crawl through the bushes, through the gate and around to the back door."

"What about the motion light, won't it turn on as we go by?"

Jonathan knew all about the light. On past occasions he had played a game with it, trying to sneak past without being detected. He realized that it was no longer a game. "Not if we move real slowly! We'll be in its range when we reach the end of the bushes," Jonathan whispered. "Let's go!"

Simon raised his voice slightly and said, "If you kids come out right now, we won't hurt you."

"Yeah, we've just got something for ya!" Marvin added.

"Boss, I can't see 'em!"

"Just keep looking, they haven't left this yard. Maybe they're under those bushes."

"Jonathan, they're coming this way!" Katie said in a strained whisper.

Jonathan and Katie had crept through the bushes and were now in range of the motion light. "If we just move slowly, the light won't turn on." Jonathan whispered back.

"Jonathan, my hair is caught on the bush!" Katie exclaimed in a loud whisper. "I can't move without shaking it."

"Katie, don't yank on the branch or you'll trigger the light!" Suddenly, a loud hissing sound startled all four of them.

"Boss, the sprinklers!" Marvin exclaimed.

"I don't care if it storms! Keep looking for those kids!" said Simon as the sprinklers pelted him.

"Katie, the sprinklers are going to trigger the motion light. Hurry. We've got to get through the gate!" Jonathan whispered.

"Jonathan, I can't get my hair free!" Katie said, frantically tugging on the branch that held her hostage.

"Katie, stay calm. Break the branch or something, just don't move too fast — the light!"

It was then that Katie noticed that the sprinkler was coming right for her. She gave one last tug to free her hair and winced at the pain, her eyes watering. "Ow!"

Just then the automatic light clicked back on.

"There they are!" shouted Simon in victory.

"Run!" cried Jonathan.

Simon caught up with Katie and clasped his hand over her mouth.

"Katie! I'll save you." Jonathan ran at Simon only to be caught by Marvin.

"Got him, boss! Stop struggling, ya little pipsqueak!" Marvin put his hand over Jonathan's mouth, muffling his screams.

"Don't move and don't make a sound," said Simon. "I told you we won't hurt you . . . yet."

"Yeah, just scare yous guys a bit," Marvin chimed in.

Simon glared at Jonathan. "What did you find in that cave?"

Marvin uncovered Jonathan's mouth to let him answer. "It's a secret that I'll never share with you!" Jonathan screamed.

Just then, the doorknob on the front door began to turn.

"Here's something for your father. Give him this note," Simon demanded, shoving an envelope at Jonathan.

"Someone's coming out!" cried Marvin.

"Let's go!" Simon exclaimed.

They ran off as Kendall came out the door. "What's taking

you so . . . ." Kendall saw the men run to the car. "Hey!" He said as the car sped off. He looked confused as his wet kids came rushing to him. "What happened to you two?"

"Dad!" Katie said with a wavering voice.

"Katie, what's going on here?" Kendall demanded out of fear.

"Dad, these two men grabbed us and told us to give this to you." Jonathan's hand was shaking as he handed the note to his dad.

"Are you two okay?" He asked bending down to look closely at his children.

"Yeah, we're okay," said Katie weakly, looking pale and wet.

"What's this?" Kendall mumbled as he looked at the envelope. "It's . . . a note!" Kendall began to read the contents out loud. "Tonight should leave no doubt in your mind that we have the power to hurt your family. Don't breathe a word of what you found in the cave to anyone. Stay away from the Brenans' farm, and your kids will be safe!"

Angela and Grandpa Benjamin joined them in the front yard. "Honey, what's going on?" Angela asked, alarmed.

"Son, who's threatening you?" asked Grandpa.

"Obviously, it was someone who doesn't want us involved with the Brenans," Kendall said.

"Why not?" Jonathan asked innocently.

"I'm not sure." Kendall thought for a minute. Then he snapped his fingers. "Someone doesn't want anyone to know how much the Brenans' farm could be worth. They probably want to buy it out from under them."

"So, now what?" asked Grandpa.

"Well, this certainly changes things!" Kendall said.

"You mean we're not going to the cave now?" Jonathan asked, disappointed.

"No, we are definitely going back! Tomorrow." Kendall replied.

"All right!" cheered Jonathan.

"Kendall . . ." Angela said with concern.

"Tomorrow?" asked Grandpa.

"Yes, I just need to remove that fossil and take some pictures. Then I'll contact a museum I know and see if they're interested in my findings. And I'll need some help," Kendall said, winking at Jonathan.

"Kendall!" Angela reproved.

"I'm with ya!" Jonathan shouted.

—•—•—

The sun was just rising over the city of Santa Fe. Dark ominous clouds were turning bright yellows and reds, and only the most brilliant morning stars were still visible. Lights from passing cars reflected off the windows of the restaurant. The smell of bacon and eggs filled the air.

Inside the restaurant, Marvin and Vinnie sat in a booth. "Marvin, where do you think Simon is?"

"I don't . . ." Marvin caught a glimpse of Simon as he came through the front door. "Ah, there he is."

Simon began to make his way past the hostess and toward their table. "Good morning, gentlemen," greeted Simon as he sat down.

Marvin looked up at him. "Boss, we were startin' to get worried about ya."

"Would you boys like to start out with something to drink?" asked a waitress as she stepped up to the table.

"Yeah, I'll take an orange . . ." Marvin was interrupted by Simon.

"We'll all have coffee, thanks!"

"Coming right up!" The waitress turned and headed back to the kitchen.

"But, boss, I hate coffee. I was gonna have orange juice!"

"How'd it go last night, boss?"

"Vinnie, let's just say the Park family must be a little shook."

"A little? We scared 'em to death!" said Marvin.

"I don't think they'll be any trouble. But just in case, I want you and Marvin to take turns watching their house. Give me a call on the cell phone if anything looks like it's going on."

"I'll take the first shift, Simon," Vinnie volunteered.

"Perfect, you can start right after breakfast."

"What about me, boss?"

"Well, Marvin, I think you and I have a little shopping to do. I wonder where someone can get explosive devices here in Santa Fe."

# 7
# Return to the Hidden Cave

The sun was hanging low in the sky as day gave way to evening. Kendall and Jonathan stood in the driveway along with Angela.

"Well, honey, we're on our way," Kendall said.

"I can't believe you're going so late in the afternoon."

"We'll be okay, Mom."

"Why are you going so late?" Angela questioned again.

"Well, like I said, we want to lie low. Obviously, someone wants us to stay away from the cave. If we leave now, by the time we meet Jessie at the cave, the sun will have set. In the dark there's less chance we'll be found out!" Kendall explained.

"Are you sure Jonathan and Jessie should go?" Angela asked once more.

"Angela, they'll do fine. We're just going down to retrieve that one fossil and take a few pictures. Besides, I can't do it without them," Kendall assured her.

"Please be careful!" Angela pleaded.

"We will," Kendall said in his most confident voice. "We're on our way!"

"I love you, Mom!"

"I love you too, honey."

Kendall turned to Angela: "We'll see you late tonight, " he said, giving a quick kiss to his wife. Then he and Jonathan climbed into the red 4x4 and started the engine.

"Purrs like a kitten. Not bad, after the last spill she took," joked Kendall.

"I can't believe Grandpa fixed it!" commented Jonathan.

About a block away sat the black Lincoln. Tinted glass hid the figure that sat inside. The figure grabbed the cell phone and dialed. "Simon?" he asked, pausing for an answer. "Simon?"

"Vinnie, where are you?" answered Simon forcefully.

"I'm just down the street from the Parks, just like you told me!" Vinnie answered.

"So, why are you calling?" Simon squawked.

"Because they're leaving!"

"Leaving?" the interest picked up in Simon's voice. "Do they have anything with them?"

"Boy, do they!" Vinnie answered, peering through his binoculars. "They've been working like little ants."

"Spare me the metaphors Vinnie. What did you see them pack?"

"I watched 'em load a rope, some kind of pulley, and it looks like a generator and some lights."

"They're heading for the cave. They've got more nerve than I bargained for. Hmm, middle class family with an attitude. How pathetic! Okay, gentlemen, it's time for Plan B, where Simon gets nasty! Vinnie, you follow far behind them. Marv and I will pick up the timed explosives and meet you there."

It was getting harder to see as Jonathan, Jessie, and Shadow stood outside the cave waiting for Kendall to come back out. Having cleared away the brush, the hole was now very visible. After what seemed like hours, Kendall emerged from the cave.

"Okay, kids. This generator," he said pointing to a large engine sitting beside the mouth of the cave, "is providing power for the temporary lights down in the cavern," Kendall explained.

"Can Shadow come, too, Dr. Park?" Jessie shouted above the noise of the generator.

"Of course," said Kendall. "He's officially one of the team."

"Maybe he could sniff out bones," said Jessie.

"Well, I'd rather have him for us than against us," muttered Jonathan.

"He doesn't bite," Jessie said defending her dog.

"All right," Jonathan said uneasily.

"This is going to be fun!" said Jessie.

"I think we're ready. I've got my pack, you two have yours. We've got tools, flashlights . . . oh, don't forget the camera and film. Let's go!"

Kendall slid down the steep incline, and Jonathan followed. "I'm right behind you, Dad. Be careful of the wires, Jessie," Jonathan called back.

"I'm okay," said Jessie a little defensively. "C'mon, Shadow."

As they descended deeper into the cave the sound of the generator faded.

"Jonathan, remember, all we have to do is get that skull and bring it back out. Oh, and take some pictures," Kendall said. "And if we've got time, let's photograph the bat."

"Oh right, simple, Dad!" Jonathan said, laughing at his dad's idea of easy.

—◆◆—

The phone rang. Thad picked up the phone. "Hello."

"Thad, this is Mike."

"Hey, what's up?"

"It's about Jonathan," Mike said.

Thad could hear the concern in his voice. "Jonathan?"

"I was watching their house from my window. . . ."

"Yeah?"

"I saw Jonathan and his dad leaving in their truck, with a bunch of stuff in it," Mike said.

"Yeah, remember? Jonathan said he and his dad were going back to the cave tonight," Thad pointed out.

"Oh, that's right . . ." Mike said, trailing off in thought.

"So, what's wrong?"

"Well, as they left, I saw a man in a black Lincoln follow them!"

"No joke?" Thad asked.

"No joke. I wonder who it was."

"Oh no!" exclaimed Thad.

"What?"

"Remember, Jonathan said those two guys showed up at their house last night?" Thad said.

"Oh, yeah. I think I saw their car . . . it was the same one!"

"Oh, man, I bet that was them! What do we do, Mike?"

"I don't know — my parents aren't here."

"Mine either. My Uncle Rob is watching me and Timmy while they're in California."

"Well, we've got to get to the cave and tell the Parks!" said Mike.

"Right! How are we going to get there?" asked Thad.

Mike thought for a moment. "How old is your uncle?"

"Eighteen."

"Does he have a car?"

"Yeah, he's cool, he'll take us!" Thad exclaimed.

"Why don't you call Eddie? You guys can pick him up on the way over here," Mike suggested.

"Deal!"

—◆◆—

"Dad, are you okay in there?" Jonathan called from the archway just outside the room with the skull. His voice echoed throughout the cave.

"Yes, I've got the skull! You and Jessie wait there! I'll be right out."

The two watched in the light powered by the generator, while he maneuvered through the stalagmites. Jessie shivered, remembering her fall the week before. Jonathan remembered it, too, and hoped he wouldn't have to try to save his dad.

"Wow, this is exciting!" exclaimed Jessie.

"I can't wait to see it," agreed Jonathan.

"Jonathan, I need a hand!" Kendall called from the room. "Can you grab the backpack from me?"

"Here you go, Dad!" Jonathan stretched out his hand and grabbed the pack.

"Be careful with that! It's got my tools and the camera," Kendall said, joining them in the main corridor. "I got some great pictures and data before I removed it. Now for a look at this thing," Kendall said, holding the fossil up to the light.

"Cool!" said Jonathan.

"It's all broken up," said Jessie. "It's not all there."

"It's been through a lot, Jessica. Actually, as fossils go, this one's in remarkable shape. And I can't believe how fortunate we are to find it."

"Is it a Coelophysis, Dad?"

"Yes, Jonathan, I'm pretty sure. This looks just like the Coelophysis fossils found at Ghost Ranch," Kendall explained.

"Cool, a real dinosaur," said Jessie.

"Dad, you said that this skull didn't belong here. Why?"

"Well, Jonathan, before we can talk about why this skull doesn't come from this cave, you need to understand how the cave and the fossil were made."

"Is this about Noah's flood?" asked Jessie.

"Yes, very much so. You see, the flood was a huge event. The Bible tells us that the entire world was covered with water. And that there were great fountains of the deep — or undersea volcanoes that erupted. It was the worst catastrophe that the world had ever seen. In the midst of all of that action, different types of rocks and mud were being moved from one place to another."

"And that's what made rock layers?" Jonathan asked.

"That's right. After the flood was over, huge layers of rock and mud stretched over many parts of the world. When geologists look at them now, the rock layers speak of a great catastrophe."

"Are there layers here in Abiquiu?" asked Jessica.

"Yes, and there are two different types that I need to explain to you. One type of layer is called limestone. Limestone usually comes from the bottom of the ocean. But we find patches of it right here in New Mexico, hundreds of miles away from the sea. Creationist scientists believe that this is evidence that the flood picked up this limy mud from the very bottom of the ocean and put it in different places around the world, where it hardened into limestone."

"Dad, isn't this cave made from limestone?" asked Jonathan.

"Exactly!" Kendall said, proud of his son. "The limestone layer was placed here by the flood. It was just a thick layer, without the cave. But later, the cave was formed when acidic waters carved out these caverns."

"So, right after the flood, this cave wasn't even here?" asked Jonathan.

"Right, that didn't happen until later," Kendall said. "Since limestone comes from the bottom of the ocean, scientists usually find fossils from sea animals, not dinosaurs, in the limestone layers. And since this cave wasn't carved until after the flood, and most dinosaurs died in the flood, I was suprised to find a Coelophysis skull here."

"So what about the other layer?" asked Jessica.

"What?"

"You said you were going to tell us about two layers."

"Oh yes," said Kendall. "The other layer of rock is known as the Chinle formation."

"Chinle? What's that?" asked Jessie.

"Well, Chinle is a layer of soft rock that stretches into northern Utah, southern Nevada, and up into Colorado. It's also very common throughout New Mexico. It has a very red color. That's why many of the cliffs around Abiquiu are so red, because they're made from this stuff. Because the Chinle covers such large areas, scientists think that it was put there by a large event like the flood. Lots of dinosaurs have been found in this layer, including the dinosaurs at Ghost Ranch."

"So, Dad, was this dinosaur killed at the same time as those dinosaurs at Ghost Ranch?" asked Jonathan.

"Yes, I think so, during the flood. You see, all of that water picked up the Chinle material, and carried it all the way into New Mexico. I'd say that some unsuspecting dinosaurs were instantly buried by tons of this Chinle. And because of all the water and mud, and the right chemical conditions, those Coelophysis were fossilized together in one huge pile. And I think that this skull tells us that this is true."

"How?" Jessica asked, as she and Jonathan moved closer to look.

"Remember that this skull is no longer made of bone. The bone has been replaced by the rock minerals that were around it when it was fossilized. See its red color? This is the same color as Chinle. That means it's probably made from minerals found in the Chinle formation. But look here. On top are some of the limestone deposits from the cave. Those must have been added after the skull was placed in the cave."

"So, Dad, how'd the skull get in here?"

"Jonathan, that's a good question, and I think the answers are all around us," Kendall answered.

"They are?" Jessie asked.

"Yeah, this is where he asks us the questions." Jonathan explained to the newest member of the adventure team.

"So, this is the mystery — how'd the skull get here? What clues do we have?" Kendall asked in a very mysterious tone.

"Well," Jessie guessed, "this cave is made from limestone."

"But the cave wasn't carved until a while after the flood," added Jonathan.

"Excellent!" said Kendall. "But what about the skull?"

"Well, you said the skull was fossilized in the Chinle formation during the flood," Jonathan reasoned.

"Yes. . . ."

"So, the dinosaur skull was in the Chinle formation before the cave was carved," Jonathan said, a little confused.

"So, what is the skull doing here?" asked Kendall.

There was a moment of silence. Then Jonathan asked, "Dad, can you give us a hint?"

"What if the skull was fossilized by the flood, and then moved into the cave after it was formed?" Kendall hinted.

"The crack in the cave!" exclaimed Jessie.

"Right!" said Kendall. "Something else like another smaller flood, or mudslide or earthquake must have carried the skull from where it was originally fossilized, and then dropped it into the cave. And it got here through that crack in the cave ceiling!" Kendall said as he pointed back to the stalagmite room. "Mystery solved!"

Meanwhile above the cave, a brown BMW pulled in behind the black Lincoln already parked near the debris of the recently fallen tree. Simon and Marvin got out and walked down to the mouth of the cave where Vinnie was waiting. "They're in the cave, boss," Vinnie said, greeting them.

"What's that thing making that awful noise, Vinnie?" Marvin asked.

"Looks like the boy and his dad have set up a generator."

"I knew it. As a paleontologist, he's trying to prove that there are fossils down there!" Simon pondered. "Marvin, did you bring the chloroform?"

"Chloroform?"

"Yesss," Simon asked with rising impatience. "The stuff that knocks them out."

"I knew that."

"Oh, right, Marv!" Vinnie teased.

"Oh, uh, of course I got the chloroform."

Vinnie hit Marv with his cap.

"Will ya stop hittin' me with that stupid hat already. Who do ya think you are wearing a hat anyway, Indiana Jones?"

Vinnie hit him again.

"Ow!"

"Would you two stop! We have work to do!" growled Simon.

"What are we going to do, boss?" asked Vinnie.

"So, Vinnie, you saw just the boy and his dad leaving the house right?'

"That's right, Boss."

"Okay, here's the plan. I'll turn off the generator. Meanwhile, Marvin will put a little chloroform on two rags and give one to Vinnie. When they come out to check on the generator, Vinnie you put the rag over the father's mouth and knock him out cold. Marvin, you get the little boy."

"Then what'll we do with 'em boss?"

"First we need to get rid of any evidence of fossils they've found. Then I'll set up timed explosives. We'll blow up this place and lock them away until we can buy this land."

"What if they still don't want to sell?"

"Don't you see, the Brenans don't know how valuable fossils are. The only other people that even know what's in the cave, much less how valuable it is, are the Parks, and they have no evidence until they produce a fossil. All we have to do is keep them quiet and destroy the evidence until the Brenans sign on the dotted line. Because if somebody does find a dinosaur fossil, then every museum in the country will want to buy this place," hissed Simon. "Now don't just stand there! Let's get to work."

Simon, Vinnie, and Marvin didn't hear the VW van coming closer on the road below them. "Okay, guys, where did you say the cave was?" asked Uncle Rob. He was in the driver's seat, and in the back seat were four boys. "I can't believe we're doing this!"

"Jonathan said it was on this dirt road," said Thad.

"There's the Lincoln!" exclaimed Mike.

"Slow down!"

"Park here!"

"No, here!" instructed the boys all at once.

"Wow, this is serious. We need to tell someone. Hey! I bet there's a car phone in that Lincoln," said Uncle Rob. "Guys, I want you to stay here. I'm going to go call the police. Whose land is this?"

"The Brenans!" They all said in unison.

"Okay," said Rob. "You guys stay put when I leave, okay? I don't want you running around in the dark. I'll be right back. Especially you two, Thad and Timmy." He closed the door quietly and crept up the road toward the other cars.

"Do you think he really meant we needed to stay here, Thad?" asked Timmy.

"Naw, he just afraid our parents will find out that he left us on our own with suspected felons around," said Thad. "But Jonathan really needs our help right now, so it's up to us to save him. Right, guys?" asked Thad.

"Right," they said in unison.

"Okay, get your flashlights and let's go."

Outside the cave, the generator went quiet as Simon flipped the switch.

"Hey, what happened to all the lights?" asked Jonathan as the cave went pitch-black.

"The generator's probably out of gas," Kendall said, flipping on his flashlight. "I need to go up and check on it. I think the two of you will be safe if you stay here. I'll be right back," said Kendall. "Do you have your flashlights?"

"Check," said Jonathan.

"I have mine, too," said Jessie, pulling it out of her pack.

"Here — switch with me, Jessie. Mine's brighter," said Kendall. After I get the generator back on, we'll finish by taking pictures of the bat," Kendall turned and began to walk toward the entrance of the cave.

Jonathan and Jessie watched Kendall's light bounce up and down as it disappeared into the distance. With only the light from the flashlight, the cave seemed very dark and lonely.

The full moon cast eerie shadows over the hillside as the Eagle's Nest gang continued to sneak toward the entrance of the cave. As they got closer, Eddie whispered to the other boys, "Guys, there's three of them."

The four boys crouched behind some nearby bushes. "What's that big thing in front of the cave?" Timmy asked.

"It's probably some type of pump that they're using to fill the cave with deadly nerve gasses!" Eddie whined.

"Duuuh! It's a generator and it's not running," Mike said.

"I hope they have flashlights," said Eddie.

"It's always something," grumbled Kendall as he emerged from the mouth of the cave. He walked right passed Vinnie hiding behind a nearby bush as he made his way to the generator. "Okay, what seems to be the problem here?" Kendall said to himself.

Suddenly Kendall felt someone grab him from behind. "Let me go!" Kendall yelled. Before he knew it, Vinnie had pinned his arms behind his back. Vinnie then slipped a rag over his mouth. Kendall tried to warn Jonathan but could only mumble through the cloth as he felt his world growing dim.

"Out like a light. You shouldn't have come here, Mr. Pahk," chided Vinnie.

"What are we gonna do with him now, boss?" asked Marvin.

"Check him for fossils!" barked Simon.

Marvin patted him down. "He's clean."

"Vinnie, follow me up to the car. You can watch over Dr. Park, and I'll get the explosives." said Simon. "Marvin, you get the kid when he comes out."

"Right, boss," said Marvin.

Vinnie hoisted the limp Kendall onto his back and began to carry him down the hill.

"Look! Those guys must be taking Mr. Park down to their car," Thad said nervously.

"I told you it was poisonous gases!" Eddie whimpered in horror.

"It is not! They just used that stuff that knocks you out for a while," Mike said.

"Thad, I'm scared!" cried Timmy.

"Timmy, it'll be okay. By the way, where is Uncle Rob?" asked Thad.

"Wasn't he going to their car?" exclaimed Mike.

"Oh, no!" They said in unison.

"Do you realize it's up to us now? Jonathan is in danger and we're his only hope," Thad shuddered.

# 8

# Simon Says

Jonathan and Jessie sat listening to the rhythmic drips of mineral water falling onto the cave floor. They jumped at each noise, hoping it was Jonathan's dad.

"Jessie, why do you think my dad's taking so long?"

"I don't know, but let's go check."

"Okay. But we better bring the fossil with us, just in case we can't get the generator back on." Jonathan grabbed his dad's backpack containing the skull and the camera.

"Let's get going, okay?" suggested Jessie.

"Yeah, okay," Jonathan said. "Where's Shadow?"

"I don't know. He wandered off while we were waiting for your dad to find the fossil. Shadow?" Jessie called, shining her light down the hallway. He was no where to be found. "Here, boy . . . Shadow?" But there was no answer. "This light is getting dimmer," Jessie said. "Augh!!! The flashlight your dad gave me went dead!"

"This place gives me the willies. I'm glad I still have my light. I'm not sure I like the thought of your dog creeping up on me."

"He doesn't bite!" insisted Jessie.

"It's sure a lot scarier in here with just one flashlight. And think of those bats," said Jessie.

"It's okay. We saw them leave. Most of them anyway. But you never know, ha ha ha," Jonathan said turning to Jessie to tease her.

"Stop it, Jonathan. Hey, look out!"

"Ahhhh, whoa!" Jonathan was suddenly sitting on the floor of the cave rubbing his head.

"Are you okay, Jonathan? I can't see. What happened?"

"I hit a stalactite and dropped the flashlight. Did you see where it fell?" Jonathan said, bending down on all fours to feel for the flashlight.

"No," Jessie answered.

"Uh-oh, I found it. Its glass is cracked, and it won't turn on."

"What should we do now?" asked Jessie. "We can't see."

"We'll just have to inch along the wall until we reach the opening, and then we can climb out and find out what's going on," said Jonathan.

———

Outside the cave, the boys were still trying to figure out how to save Jonathan.

"Hey, I've got an idea," said Mike. "If we could just get those guys to leave the entrance of the cave for a couple of minutes, we could sneak down into the cave and get Jonathan. Hopefully, by the time we come up, Rob will be here with help!"

"So, how are we going to get them away from the cave?" asked Thad.

"We need a diversion. Eddie, have you still got those firecrackers?" Mike asked.

"Right here in my pocket."

"Okay. Eddie, I want you to light the whole pack and throw it as far into those bushes as possible," said Mike. "When they leave to see what it is, we'll sneak quickly up into the cave."

"Got your flashlights?" Thad asked. They all nodded.

"Okay, nobody use 'em until we get into the cave. All right?" asked Thad.

They all nodded . . . except Eddie who was still rummaging through his pocket. He pulled out his jawbreaker, pocketknife, and then his watch and checked the time. "Gee guys, if I was home right now, I'd just about be having my nine-o'clock snack."

"Come on, Eddie, forget about food! Have ya got the firecrackers or not?" Mike snapped.

"Yeah, they're right here. Oh, and here's my lighter, too."

"Light those things and chuck them as far as you can!" Thad said.

"Here goes nothin'." Eddie lit the whole pack of firecrackers and grunted as he threw them deep into the bushes.

The firecrackers exploded, shattering the silence of the night.

"What's that, boss?" Marvin yelled, startled.

"I don't know, but it came from over there," Simon said, pointing in the direction of the noise.

"It sounded like gunshots!"

"No, it wasn't gunshots, but someone's over there. Now, follow me," ordered Simon.

"I don't believe it!" whispered Mike. "It worked!"

"Okay, everyone, let's head to the mouth of the cave very, very quickly and quietly," Thad directed, "Let's go!"

Thad, Mike, and Eddie moved quickly toward the cave. None of them noticed that Timmy wasn't moving. "We're almost there," whispered Mike. "We're gonna' make it."

"Wait. Where's Timmy?" Thad asked, his voice getting a little tense. "Where's my little brother?"

"I don't know!" Mike whispered, concerned.

Then the boys stopped dead in their tracks. A loud beeping sound cut through the night air.

"Eddie, it's your watch!" Thad yelled in a whisper.

"Turn it off, Eddie!" Mike whispered threateningly.

Eddie was already rummaging through his pocket. "I can't find it guys! Guys, we're in deep trouble! They're going to use that nerve gas on us!"

"Eddie . . ." Mike began, but never finished.

"Welcome to our little party, gentlemen," Simon said, out of breath from his run.

"Yeah, we welcome youse guys to the pahty." Marvin repeated. "We've already caught one of yous guys usin' the phone in our cahr."

"Oh no — Uncle Rob!" cried Thad.

"My associate, Marvin here, is going to escort you down to the car. If you give him any trouble, he's got a little treat for you," Simon threatened.

"A treat?" Eddie's ears perked up.

"Eddie!" reproved Mike.

"Should I take 'em now, boss?" Marvin asked.

Eddie dropped to his knees and started wailing. "No! No! I don't wanna die. I'm too young to die."

"Oh, pah-lease. Marvin, take them down to the car and leave them with Vinnie. Then come back up to the cave."

Eddie was still on the ground. "We're not going to die? Oh, thank you! Thank you," he said, bowing low and kissing Simon's feet repeatedly.

"Eddie, get up!" whispered Thad.

"Enough!" said Simon. "Get these kids out of here!"

"Right, boss!" said Marvin.

"What's taking that Park boy so long? Why hasn't he surfaced yet?" fumed Simon, as Marvin rounded up the boys. "I'm going in after him. Give me some of that chloroform."

"Okay, but that stuff will knock you out."

"Not for me, you imbecile," said Simon.

⚫⚫

Back in total darkness, Jessie and Jonathan were inching blindly along the wall toward the entrance of the cave.

"Okay, Jessie, we just need to keep moving."

"It's just so dark. It makes me nervous. And where's Shadow?" Jessie said and then called out for her dog.

"He's probably waiting around some dark corner so he can ambush me from behind!" Jonathan said.

"No, he's not!"

In the distance, a ray of light sliced through the darkness.

"Look, there's Dad now with the flashlight!"

"Then why didn't he turn on the generator?" Jessie whispered suspiciously.

"It's probably out of gas. Da—!" Before Jonathan finished calling out to his father, Jessica clamped her hand over his mouth.

"Sh," Jessie said quietly, "I'm not so sure it's him."

"What do you mean? Who else would it be?"

"I don't know! It just doesn't feel right," she said, trying to pinpoint the reason she felt uneasy.

"That's right! Dad used your light, and it was going dim.

That one's really bright and big. That's not Dad."

"Exactly!" Jessie said triumphantly.

"Something's wrong. We better hide," whispered Jonathan. "Let's get moving, because that light is coming closer."

"How? We can't see anything?" As Jessie was talking, the light bounced off of the cave wall next to her. Jonathan began taking a few steps back, but his backpack bumped into the wall with a loud thump.

Instantly the beam of light snapped to Jonathan who found himself squinting into its bright glare. "Who's there?" he asked, his voice shaking.

Simon's voice rang through the cave. "Well, well, if it isn't Mr. Jonathan Park."

Jonathan felt goose bumps as he recognized the sinister voice from last night's scare. His heart beat wildly as the details from the previous night's attack played back in his mind. The sound of loose rocks jolted him back to the present. It was Jessie's footsteps as she tried to inch away into the darkness. Panic gripped Jonathan as he realized that Simon could probably hear her. To cover the noise, Jonathan rubbed his backpack along the cave and began to ask, "What are you doing?" Simon whipped his flashlight quickly to the left, revealing Jessie with her hands up along the cave wall, feeling her way to the back of the cave.

"There's two of you, are there?" Simon sneered. "Ah, aren't you the Brenans' little girl? With you in hand, your parents will be sure to sign on the dotted line."

"Run!" yelled Jonathan.

"Running away, aye? Not very smart, boy," said Simon, breaking into a stride.

"I can't see!" said Jessie.

"Neither can I!" Jonathan said running beside her. As they ran, the flashlight beam from Simon's light bounced up and down behind them, casting their shadows on walls as Simon chased them. Occasionally the beam provided valuable glimpses of the cave terrain as the two continued as fast as they could.

"Jonathan, if we keep running, we may trip over another hidden cliff!"

"Jessie, if we don't keep running he's going to get us. And

believe me, he's even scarier close up. We've got to keep going!"

Behind them, a winded Simon was catching up. The flashlight was giving him an unfair advantage. "If you stop now, I won't hurt you."

"Where's your dog when we need him?" Jonathan puffed.

"I don't know, do you think Simon got him?"

"He was probably smart and went home!"

Jonathan's shoelace had come loose and caught on a large rock. He was suddenly propelled forward. He hit the ground with a thud. "Ooofff!"

"Jonathan!" Jessie called out. "Are you okay?"

"I tripped, and I think I skinned my knee. My ankle is killing me. Go Jessie, don't wait for me — don't let him get you!"

"Not without you. C'mon," she said, yanking him up.

"Jessie, we need to get this backpack to Dad. Its got the only evidence of the fossils."

"You fools, I've almost got you! Quit running and make it easy on all of us!" taunted Simon from only 30 feet away.

Although his ankle was killing him, Simon's taunt was all the motivation Jonathan needed to continue running. "I think the cave turns to the right," said Jonathan. Just around the corner they could barely make out the outline of a rock formation. They stopped to catch their breath. "Let's hide behind these rocks."

As Simon huffed around the corner, he no longer heard them running. He stopped, listened for a moment, and then shined his flashlight all around the cave.

From behind the rocks, Jessie and Jonathan held their breath. Finally, once again they heard his footsteps echoing throughout the cave, each step bringing him closer. Soon they saw the light sweeping the room, edging nearer to their hiding place.

Jonathan unzipped his coat, carefully rolled it up and wrapped it around his waist.

"Jonathan, what are you doing?" Jessie whispered.

"I'm just putting my coat around my waist!"

"Someone's after us, and you're worried about being hot? Shh! He'll find us," warned Jessie.

Simon stopped. "Trying to hide from me? Well, you might as well give up. We already have your father."

"They've got Dad!" Jonathan whispered.

"Still not coming out? There's no other way out you know," said Simon, shining his light right over the rocks they were hiding behind. They both held their breath. Then Simon began walking.

"He walked past us!" said Jessie.

"Jessie, he doesn't know for sure there's no other way out."

"Jonathan, where are you and your little friend? I'm getting very tired of this game," Simon yelled out angrily. "Look, you can stay in here for all I care. All I want is any evidence of fossils. Do you have pictures? Give them to me, and you may keep your life!"

"What are we going to do now?" Jessie asked.

"We need to find that hollow room."

"Where all the bats are? Why?" asked Jessie horrified.

"Because they may. . . ."

"You love games, aye? How about 'Simon Says'? Simon says that we have exactly 15 minutes to get out of this cave. You see, I've set timed explosives at the entrance of the cave. I'm going to seal this place so no one will ever believe you found fossils here. I'm only going to look a few minutes more before I leave you here with the rest of the fossils!"

"He's gonna blow us up! We've got to find Shadow and get out of here!" said Jessie in a frantic whisper.

"Let's go!" They followed just behind Simon, using the light of his flashlight to guide them.

"Simon says ka boom! Ha ha ha!" Simon slowed almost to a stop.

They squatted down against the side of the cave.

Then Simon turned off his flashlight so Jessie and Jonathan couldn't see him.

"Why did he turn off his light?" whispered Jessie as they huddled together in the jet-blackness of the cave. "How are we going to find the hollow room in the dark? And where's Shadow?"

"I don't know. If only we had a light!" said Jonathan.

"Dear Lord, please give us light!" Jessie prayed, then turned toward Jonathan. "I think it's to the right."

"No, Jessie, it's to the left," Jonathan said, tugging on Jessica's shirtsleeve.

Suddenly, Simon jumped out of nowhere! "Gottcha!" Simon

shouted, grabbing Jonathan from behind. "Hey, Jonathan, remember me?" He flipped the flashlight on and pointed it up to his face. The long shadows made his fiendish features look even more evil.

"Augh!" Jessie gasped. "You know the light on your face like that isn't very flattering."

"Let me go!" said Jonathan, grabbing at Simon's arm, which was wrapped tightly around Jonathan's neck.

"Jessie, run, he's got me!"

# 9
# Out of
# Time

Back at the car, Marvin was arriving with the boys. "Hey, Vinnie, look what I've got . . . three more."

"Where'd they come from?" asked Vinnie.

"Friends of the kid's, I guess."

"Marvin, I'll take care of them. You get back to the cave and check on Simon."

"I'm on my way!" said Marvin.

As Vinnie shoved the kids into the car, they sat in the back seat with Uncle Rob. In the front seat laid the unconscious body of Kendall Park. "Rob! Uncle Rob, what are you doing here?" asked Thad in disbelief.

"I thought I told you guys to stay in the car!" scolded Rob.

"Well, I'm sorry," said Thad with sincere apology in his voice. "Our friend was in trouble. But, weren't you going to be the one to go for help?"

"I was calling on their cell phone when this big ape came up from behind carrying the limp guy. I didn't see 'em until he was on me!"

"Did you get ahold of the Brenans?" Thad whispered in secret.

"Yes."

"Uncle Rob, little Timmy is missing!" Thad whispered. "We

don't know where he is. He's the only one that hasn't been caught!"

Little Timmy crouched down by the generator, remembering that this was what made it light in the cave. "This is for you, Jonathan." Timmy reached over and began frantically flipping switches, trying to start the generator, realizing that the three men could be back at any time.

＊＊

"Let me go, Simon!" Jonathan's yell echoed throughout the cave.

"Owww! You brat, stop kicking!" Simon growled. "So, what do we have in this backpack of yours?" Simon pulled the pack from Jonathan's shoulder.

"Leave my pack alone!" he said, grabbing for it.

"I bet there's some very important items in this pack. It would be a terrible shame to lose them after all of this work!" Simon laughed as he grappled to hold Jonathan and unzip the backpack so he could see inside.

"Give it back!" For a moment Jonathan thrust his hand into the pack. He felt the plastic case of what felt like a camera. He pulled it from the pack, and held it up. "Jessie, I've got the camera!"

"Correction, I've got the camera," gloated Simon. "You've only got the flash! Give it to me!"

"Okay, here goes. Say cheese!" Jonathan said, flipping the switch. The bright light blinded Simon. As he blinked from the flash, the entire cave was filled with bright light. "Now that's a long flash!" Jonathan exclaimed.

"It's not the flash — the generator's back on!" said Simon.

The three paused for a moment, realizing that they were right next to the cathedral. Then Jonathan kicked Simon in the shin.

"You're making me mad!" yelled Simon.

Jessie looked around. "Jonathan, we're right next to the hollow room!"

Marvin stood at the mouth of the cave. "Hey, somebody turned on this generatah'! I better get this thing back off before Simon gets mad." He reached down and killed the generator engine.

"The lights — they're back off!" exclaimed Jessie.

"Jessie, pound on the wall!" Jonathan called out as he struggled with Simon.

"Why?"

"Just trust me!"

"It's time to give up, Jonathan Park!" jeered Simon. "We're running out of time."

"Okay, here goes . . ." Jessie said, cringing. She pounded on the wall with all of her might.

Suddenly, the room was once again filled with black bats screeching and dipping in a confused mass!

"Uh! Get away from me, you wretched creatures," yelled Simon as bats swarmed around him in the dimness of his flashlight.

From out of the darkness, a growl sounded. Then out of nowhere Simon felt sharp teeth sink into his behind. "Ow! He bit me!"

Simon turned and faced Shadow, who crouched in front of him baring his teeth and growling.

"Good job, Shadow! I knew he could bite someone," said Jonathan.

"We're running out of time here, kids," said Simon.

"No, you're running out of time. We're out of here." Jonathan ran, pushing the button on his camera flash. "Here's the flash, Jessie. Light the way and follow the bats!"

The two began running after the bats. They skirted along the pit that Jessie had fallen into before. She used bursts from the flash to light their way. The sound of flapping wings and high-pitched screeching was echoing all around them. They felt the air currents as the bats swarmed around their bodies.

"It's a dead end!" said Jessie as she triggered the flash again.

"Yeah, but there's got to be a hole somewhere. The bats are disappearing through the wall."

Jessie let out a whistle, calling Shadow. Within minutes he bounded up the path and started digging at the wall.

"Good boy! Find an opening for us."

Shadow soon had made the hole big enough to wiggle through. "All right! There it is! Go ahead, boy." Dim light from the night sky was filtering through the seam in the cave. Shadow squeezed through the hole and made it out into the night.

"It's so small, I don't think we'll fit," said Jonathan, digging at the hole.

Jessie and Jonathan were startled by a burst of laughter from behind them. As they turned, they saw Simon holding the backpack into the air. "Forgetting something?" He taunted.

"Oh no, Jonathan, he's still got the backpack! We've got to get it!"

"Without the evidence in this pack, no one will ever believe that there are fossils in this cave. The Brenans will have no way to save their farm. I think I see the perfect place for it. How about the bottom of this huge pit." Simon laughed as he hurtled the pack with all of his might over the edge. Jonathan and Jessie watched in horror as Simon shined his light on the pack all the way down.

"Noooo!" yelled Jonathan, his voice rebounding through the cave.

"Jonathan! The backpack!" exclaimed Jessie.

"Simon says, goodbye evidence. Now to get out of here. Ha ha! I'm leaving you, Jonathan Park! Your bones can rest with the fossils you love so much. You've got four minutes until the explosion. Enjoy them." Simon smiled with evil pleasure.

"Jonathan, we lost the pack! How are we going to save the farm?" Jessica cried out in utter defeat.

"Jessie, the cave is about to explode. Let's worry about all that stuff later."

"You're right," said Jessie.

"We've got to squeeze through that hole. Let's go!"

The two rushed to the end of the tunnel and paused momentarily in front of the crack in the wall.

"Ah, so there is another way out!" Simon began to rush toward them.

"Let's hope we fit," Jonathan said as he began to squeeze through. "It's a tight fit, but I think we've got it!"

"Jonathan, Simon is coming right behind us!"

Jonathan felt the cool air of the night as he squeezed through the tiny hole. "Okay, Jessie, I'm out! Now it's your turn."

Jessie popped out of the cave, "We're out!"

"You'll be sorry!" yelled Simon, poking his head out of the cave.

"Jonathan, he's coming after us!"

"And I'm. . ." Suddenly the tone in Simon's voice changed, "I'm . . . I'm stuck! I can't move!"

"Ha! Ha!" Jonathan rejoiced, "He can't get out, he's too big!"

"Marvin, help me!" yelled Simon. "Marvin, where are you? They're getting away." Marvin was too far away to hear.

Shadow kept his post and growled at Simon.

For the first time in hours Jonathan and Jessie breathed the fresh air of the evening. They both realized they had been hearing a pulsating sound. They looked up to see a helicopter hovering over head. A spotlight shown down from above. In the distance they heard police sirens getting closer.

From above, through a megaphone, a voice echoed in the darkness. "This is the New Mexico Police. We want everyone to stay right where you are!"

"I don't think Simon will have any problem with that," joked Jonathan.

The helicopter came to rest right next to Jonathan and Jessie. Three men in uniform jumped out of the chopper and ran straight for them. One of the officers flashed his light on Jonathan. "What's going on? Where's Simon Addleman?"

"He's stuck in the cave over there and he can't move! He's put timed explosives at the mouth of the cave. We've only got about three more minutes!"

"Odeski, Murdock, grab the rescue foam and pull that man out, ASAP!" ordered the officer.

His radio sprang to life with a hiss, "Chief, we've apprehended two other suspects. They held five persons hostage."

The chief grabbed his radio, and squeezed the transmit button, "We've got trouble, we've got timed explosives at the mouth of the cave, T equals minus two minutes, 50 seconds and counting."

"The fossils!" yelled Jessie. "The explosion will seal the cave!"

The chief continued on the radio, "I want everyone away from the mouth of that cave, NOW!"

"Roger!"

Just a short way back, Simon was yelling from his snare. Only his head and shoulders stuck out from the cave. His arms and body were crammed into the small hole. "Get meeee outta here!"

The two officers raced toward him, carrying a container. "Quit whining. We'll have you out in a second!"

The officers pointed a thick hose at the opening. White foam came oozing out. "This ought to help you slide right out!"

"No, you idiots!" The lather muffed Simon's cry. As the officers worked to remove Simon, Shadow licked the lather off his face.

Jonathan and Jessie saw flashlights and outlines of people calling and motioning to them as they neared the road. One man wearing a uniform called out over the bullhorn, "You two need to get away from that area as quickly as possible. Run!"

"C'mon Shadow!" cried Jessie.

Within moments Shadow was running right beside them.

As Jonathan neared the blockade, one figure looked familiar. "Dad! Dad! You're alive!"

"Jonathan! I'm so glad you're okay." Kendall was now out of the car and just beginning to feel like himself.

"Everybody behind the squad cars!" yelled one officer. They all ran behind the vehicles and hunched down.

"I'm so sorry to have left you all alone in that cave. I had no idea," Kendall said, huddling next to Jonathan.

"It's okay, Dad, we made it. It's like you always say, God was still in control."

As the others joined them, Jonathan saw Angela. "Mom, what are you doing here?"

"When I got the call from the Brenans, I jumped in the car and made tracks here."

"The Brenans? Do they know what's going on?"

"They're right over there!" Angela motioned to Jessie's parents, who were running toward them.

"Mom, Dad!" Jessie cried.

"Jessica! Jonathan! I'm so glad to see you. I thought the cave had already blown up with you two in it!" said Martha hugging first Jessie then Jonathan.

"I'm okay, Mom. We found another way out and Shadow helped us," said Jessie.

"Good boy, Shadow," said Jim.

"Yeah, he bit Simon right in the behind," said Jessie.

"He bit someone?" asked Martha in horror.

Just then, four boys and a teenager walked up to the group. "Hey, hey! It's the Eagle's Nest to the rescue!" Thad proclaimed.

"Hey, guys, you're here, too?" Jonathan exclaimed.

"Mike is the one that tipped us off to everything," said Thad. "Thanks, Mike."

"Yeah, well, it was my fireworks that distracted them!" said Eddie.

"Yeah, and it was your watch that almost killed us!" Mike said.

"Without you guys, we'd be dead!" Jonathan said with great gratitude.

"It's nice to know you have such good friends, isn't it, Jonathan," Angela said pointedly.

The Brenans, Angela, and the Eagle's Nest gang clustered around Jessie, Jonathan, and Kendall, trying to piece together the story.

"Mom, the lights came on at just the right time," said Jessie. "It was like God answered my prayer."

"I turned on the lights," said Timmy proudly.

"This is my brother, Timmy the hero," said Thad.

Just then the ground shook violently. Their bodies felt the sound before their ears could make sense of it. It was a huge explosion! The shockwave traveled all the way through the cave, to the very end, causing dirt and rocks to shoot out the small hole that previously held Simon. Then, the soil around the hole collapsed back in, sealing the opening.

"The cave!" cried Kendall. "They blew up the the cave!"

"I can't believe it!" Jessie cried out. "We would've had the proof we needed, but Simon stole the backpack with the skull and tossed it into a bottomless pit!"

"But I . . ." Jonathan was cut off by his father.

"I didn't want to tell you until it was final, but I had a museum ready to buy the skull and to provide a team of diggers. But without some type of proof, it's going to take a while — too long I'm afraid — before someone is going to believe us." Discouragement fell on Kendall's face.

"Dad. . . ."

"That's all right. I'm just glad they got the bad guys," said Martha.

"Speaking of bad guys, there's Simon now. He looks like a big ball of shaving cream," chuckled Jonathan. Simon was being taken to a squad car.

"Well, if it isn't a reunion of the cave people and friends," Simon said spitting out the foam in his mouth. He was handcuffed and followed by Marvin and Vinnie with policemen on either side. As the policeman opened the squad car door for him, Simon yelled over to the group, "It's such a pity you lost your evidence down there. What do you think of your great fossil finds now? I may not have gotten your land, Jim Brenan, but at least now it's worthless. Ha! Ha! Ha! Simon says better luck next time."

"You should talk about luck, you oversized marshmallow!" Mike sneered.

"Yeah, ya giant s'more," added Eddie.

"Eddie and food . . ." Mike remarked. The whole gang laughed at the once-sinister Simon.

"Get in the car," the policeman ordered, frustrated with Simon. "It's a good thing you got used to that cave. It looks like you'll be spending quite a while in a dark lonely place."

"Ouch!!" said Simon as he sat in the car. "Don't you have a cushion or something? I'm injured. I want to speak to my lawyer." Simon's demands were cut off as the policeman closed the door.

"I overheard the police, " Angela explained. "It sounds like you aren't Simon's first victims. He's conned several families out of their homes. They've been looking for him for over a year."

"I'm glad Simon didn't get away with anything. The only problem is that he was the only real buyer for our land and the foreclosure is looming," said Jim.

"Oh, Jim," Martha sniffed, trying to keep her composure, "we've lost everything!"

"It's okay, honey," Jim said, hugging her. "We have the most important thing." He whispered in her ear, "Jessie."

"If only we had something to prove that fossil is really down there," Kendall moaned.

Jonathan began untying his jacket. He carefully unrolled it and pulled out an oblong object.

"Jonathan tried really hard," Jessie said, "but the bomb was about to go off and. . . ."

"You mean something like this skull?" Jonathan said. "And this film?" he said, pulling a black canister from his pocket.

"Jonathan, you've got the skull!" Kendall shouted in victory.

"How did you do that?" asked Jessie.

"Remember when we were hiding from Simon behind those rocks?"

"Yeah?"

"I opened the camera and pulled out the film. And then I took the skull out of the backpack. I put the film in my pocket, and I wrapped the skull up in my coat. I wasn't going to leave that thing twice."

"Then why were you so upset when Simon threw the backpack over the pit?"

"Because it had all Dad's tools in it!"

The entire group chuckled, mostly with relief that all was well.

"Our farm! This means we can keep our farm, right?" Martha exclaimed.

"But what about the fact that the cave is sealed shut?" asked Jessie.

"Well, that's the beauty of it all. If Simon had done his homework, he'd have found out that the fossil in the cave was just a fluke. Most of the fossils should be found somewhere up on the hill. We just needed some evidence to begin, and Jonathan here has provided us with it. We'll start looking on Monday!" Kendall explained.

"I'm so happy!" Martha exclaimed, "Tomorrow, after church, you're all invited to our wonderful, water-stained house to celebrate!"

Cling, cling, cling. Jim tapped on a glass. "Your attention, please. I want to say a special thanks to our guests on this Sunday afternoon. Kendall Park and Jonathan — thank you for saving us. Without you, we literally wouldn't have a roof over our heads."

"Here, here," said Martha.

"Let's thank the Lord for that," said Kendall, "I talked to the director of a museum who was very interested. If all goes well, we'll have a team ready to begin excavating immediately."

"Yeah, one look at those photos and the skull, and they'll be believers!" Jonathan chimed in.

"Amen to that. Who would have ever thought the Lord would turn this awful flood into such a blessing," said Martha.

"And you boys from the Eagle's Nest. Thank you for all you did to save these guys."

"Aw, it was nothing," said Thad.

"Well, almost nothing," added Mike. "We spent most of our time in the car."

"Hey, we tried," said Eddie.

"You all did a fine job," said Martha.

"And thank everyone for coming, so we could have ice cream for desert!" said Ryan.

"I agree!" said Jonathan.

"Mom, can we be excused?" asked Jessie. "I'd like to show these guys around."

"Sure."

All the kids clamored into the living room and filtered through the front door. Outside, in front of them, stretched all of the Brenans' property, devastated by the flood. From the front porch Jessie pointed out the worst points. Shadow was there to greet them all. "Boy, we have our own evidence of what a flood can do. See, the flood completely destroyed our barn!" said Jessie.

"Were all of your animals killed except Shadow?" asked Katie, petting the dog.

"Not all of them," said Jessica with tears in her eyes, "but some of the most special ones." The lump was getting bigger in her throat.

"Like our moo moo Molly cow," added Ryan.

Jessie looked down at her feet, trying to blink away the tears.

Inside the house, Jim and Kendall sat at the table talking. "Kendall, can I have a word with you?"

"Sure, Jim."

"Well, I've been thinking about what you said about there being no funds for creationists to buy fossils."

"Yeah?" Kendall said with rising interest.

"If your hunch is right, and there are more fossils on the land, I've been thinking about building our own creation museum."

"I'd love that," said Kendall.

"And after that, we may even make that cave safe and turn it into a tourist attraction. And with that and some backers, we could pay people like you to continue making finds that support creation."

"What a great idea," Kendall said with conviction.

"I hope and pray that it is. But most of all, I want to see this whole place work for the glory of our Creator," said Jim.

"Me, too, Jim," agreed Kendall.

Outside, the kids were sitting on the steps talking loudly. Then, suddenly, they all heard something. From around the side of the house they heard a clanking bell, and then a "mooooooo." Jessie jumped to her feet! "It's Molly!"

"Molly?" asked Katie, as the whole gang jumped up and followed after Jessie.

"Molly, their cow!" Jonathan explained.

"Molly . . ." mimicked Ryan.

They came around the corner just in time to see Jessie throw her arms around the cow. "Oh, Molly B, it is you! You're alive!"

"Molly's back!" said Ryan, clapping his hands.

"The cow? Is this a Kodak moment or what?" Thad asked.

"Don't ask me. I guess it's really tough to get friends out here," said Eddie.

"Eddie, they thought they lost her in the flood," said Mike, exasperated.

"Jonathan and Katie, guys, meet our miracle cow, Molly B," said Jessie, hugging her tightly around the neck.

"She's cute," said Katie.

"Cute?" said Mike.

"Yeah, I like her," agreed Jonathan.

"Me, too," said Ryan.

"Can I pet her?" asked Katie.

"Sure, go ahead," said Jessie. "Somehow, she survived the awful flood! She's our little cow who can remind us that there are always new tomorrows."

"She's like a rainbow," said Jonathan.

Katie picked Ryan up and he put his chubby hands on Molly

B's side. "Wanna pet the cow, Ryan?" said Katie.

"Hey, guys, wanna see if we can find some more caves?" asked Jessie.

"Yeah!" the group said unison.

"Okay, let me go ask my mom." Jessie ran back into the house with everyone tagging behind.

Jonathan ran over to his mom. "Mom, can Jessie and the gang and I go exploring? It's daylight, you know."

"Jonathan, c'mere for a minute," said Angela as she walked into the living room, away from the others. Jonathan followed.

"Mom, how come we're in the living room?" Jonathan said, a little confused and embarrassed.

"Jonathan, I just want you to stop and look around you. . . ."

"Huh?"

"Jonathan, you did it! You've made friends, and they love you."

"What do you mean?"

"Jonathan, that little gang of yours, the Eagle's Nest, they all risked their lives to save you. They're just waiting for the next adventure. And what about Jessie? She has certainly become your best friend. Jonathan Park, you've done it! You have true friends!"

Jonathan's smile was as big on the inside as it was on his face. Then he said, "Yeah, Mom, you're right. And it feels good!"

"Now go. Have fun with your friends."

Jonathan shot out of the room. "I can go!"

"Me, too!" said Jessie.

"See ya, Katie," said Jonathan as he and Jessica headed out the door.

"C'mon, Shadow."

Shadow bounded off the steps and caught up to them.

"Bye, Katie," said Jessie.

"See ya," said Mike.

"Wouldn't wanna be ya," said Eddie.

"Yeah," yelled Thad.

"You're doing a great job taking care of Ryan, Katie," teased Jonathan.

"Wait! Where are you going?" demanded Katie, still holding Ryan.

"Bye-bye, Jessie," cooed her little brother.

"How come they get to have all the fun?" Katie asked herself, watching them from the front yard.

A great field stretched in front of them. Jonathan and Jessie ran down the hill, ahead of the others. Shadow ran beside them. They paused underneath the blue sky, waiting for the rest of the gang to catch up. White clouds floated above them, the quiet stream

wound around the bend, and tall, layered rock formations stretched before them. Shadow ran around them, snapping at butterflies. "Jonathan, I'm glad we're friends," whispered Jessie, standing in the tall grass.

Jonathan looked out over the horizon filled with the excitement of future adventures. He looked back at the boys from the Eagle's Nest and then at Jessie. A slow smile crept across his face, "Me, too!" he said. "Me, too!"

# THE CREATION ADVENTURE SERIES

The biblical creation story is clearly told in the first few chapters of the Book of Genesis, and it is that story which provides the backdrop for this series. These true stories make excellent family reading — packed with high adventure and facts surrounding the events. Highlights the personal faith of the characters, and the undeniable work of the Creator's hand.

$5.95 each